Barbara Cartland

Conquered by Love

CONQUERED BY LOVE
A Bantam Book | October 1976

ISBN 0–553–02987–8

Published simultaneously in the United States and Canada

Bantam Books are published by Bantam Books, Inc. Its trade-
mark, consisting of the words "Bantam Books" and the por-
trayal of a bantam, is registered in the United States Patent
Office and in other countries. Marca Registrada, Bantam
Books, Inc., 666 Fifth Avenue, New York, New York 10019.

CONQUERED BY LOVE

Theola would have done anything to get out of England, but escape was proving more confining, more dangerous than her former prison.

She had always been nothing more than a glorified Cinderella—a poor little cousin who waited hand-and-foot on the elegant young Lady Catherine Bourne.

But now Lady Catherine had left England and was sailing through the Adriatic on her way to marry the king of Kavōnia. And Theola was sailing with her! She was free at last!

But when the ship docked in the Kavōnian harbor, Theola's new-found freedom vanished as quickly as the morning mist. The peaceful little kingdom was under seige, its imperious monarch overthrown by his own people.

And before she had time to unpack Lady Catherine's bags, Theola found herself in an empty palace guarded by the fiery, handsome man who had led the revolution—the passionate and unpredictable conqueror of Kavōnia.

BARBARA CARTLAND

Bantam Books by Barbara Cartland
Ask your bookseller for the books you have missed

CONQUERED
BY LOVE

CHAPTER ONE
1873

'I am here! I am here!' Theola thought, and only with difficulty prevented herself from crying it out aloud.

It had seemed somehow impossible, even after they had left England, that she would eventually arrive in Kavōnia.

The ship which had carried them from Marseilles had now docked safely and she could see on the Quayside a large number of impressive dignitaries waiting to receive Catherine.

To Theola it had seemed like a miracle that she had been permitted to travel with her Uncle, the Duke of

Wellesbourne, and her cousin, Lady Catherine Bourne, on a journey which was to end in Catherine becoming the Queen of Kavōnia.

Theola was well aware that it was not because her relations had any affection for her that she had been included in the party.

It was in fact simply because they could not find anyone more suitable to consent to act as Lady-in-Waiting to Catherine.

The parents of her cousin's contemporaries who might have thought it an honour to be offered such a position had declined firmly. They told the Duke they had no intention of sending their daughters to such a remote country when there was so much unrest in Europe.

"Frightened fools!" the Duke had growled as he opened letter after letter at the breakfast-table.

Each reply to his invitation made the same excuse, that they did not consider Kavōnia a sufficiently safe or attractive place for their daughters to spend two or three years of their young lives.

"I sincerely hope the country *is* quiet," the Duchess said from the other end of the table.

"Of course it is!" the Duke asserted. "As you well know, Adelaide, Kavōnia, like Montenegro, has been an independent State for many years, and now that things have settled down in Greece under King George, there is no reason to be apprehensive for Ferdinand's sovereignty. After all, he has already reigned for twelve years without any trouble."

The Duchess was silent and Catherine exclaimed almost petulantly:

"I have no wish to go into any danger, Papa! I could not bear the noise of gunfire."

"The Kavōnians are noted for their fighting ability, which is why the Ottoman Empire discreetly left them alone," the Duke replied. "The country is very mountainous and it would require an enormous Army to conquer Kavōnia, involving a huge loss of men."

"The Turks conquered Albania," Theola remarked.

2

"I am well aware of that, Theola," her Uncle said coldly, "and when I require information from you I will ask for it!"

"I am sorry, Uncle Septimus."

"What we must really concern ourselves with is to find someone who will accompany Catherine," the Duchess remarked. "She must have a Lady-in-Waiting and we have already asked everyone who seems at all suitable."

The Duke's thin lips tightened.

If there was anything he disliked it was being thwarted or refused something which he desired.

A forceful, positive man, he had a streak of cruelty in his nature which made him exceptionally harsh in his treatment of those weaker than himself.

Glancing at him, Theola thought apprehensively that because he was annoyed she was bound soon to be punished severely for some minor fault, merely so that her Uncle could relieve his feelings of frustration.

"Suppose we ask Lord Pierrepoint's daughter?" the Duchess ventured. "She is not a girl for whom I have any liking, since I consider her fast and somewhat bold in her manner, but doubtless the Pierrepoints would appreciate our condescension in inviting her to accompany Catherine."

"I will have no more refusals!" the Duke said angrily. "I have decided that Theola shall accompany Catherine."

"Theola?"

The Duchess echoed the name, her voice rising in astonishment.

"Theola?" Catherine said. "But surely, Papa . . ."

"I want no arguments—I have made up my mind," the Duke said, rising to his feet. "Theola will accompany Catherine and me to Kavōnia, and she will stay there until someone more suitable is found to take her place."

Theola had held her breath.

She could hardly believe what she had heard!

She was also desperately afraid that if she made any

3

remark which might annoy her Uncle he would change his mind.

Only after a day of excitement and bewilderment did she go down on her knees when she reached her bed-room at night and thank God for her Uncle's decision.

"I am going to Kavōnia, Papa," she added into the darkness. "Do you know, and are you glad? It is not Greece but it is very near, and the people are mostly of Greek origin. Oh, Papa, how I wish you could be with me!"

She felt as she knelt beside her bed that her father had heard her and was somehow near her, just as in moments of misery and despair she would believe that her mother was holding her close and comforting her.

There had been many moments like that since her parents had died and she had come to live with her Uncle and Aunt at the cold, cheerless Castle in Wiltshire, where the Duke had a vast Estate.

One of the richest men in England, he was also one of the meanest, and the Duchess, who before her marriage had been Her Serene Highness Adelaide of Holtz-Melderstein, was also frugal and cheese-paring in her ways.

Theola in her new home found less material comforts than she had enjoyed in the small cottage where she had lived with her mother and father before they died.

Sometimes, when she shivered with cold in the big, unheated rooms, she wished she had died with them, feeling that the bleakness and unhappiness was like black ice encompassing her until there was no warmth left in her body.

But it was not only bodily that she suffered in Wellesbourne Castle, there was the mental cruelty that she was forced to endure day in and day out until, like a frightened animal, she wanted to hide herself away from further suffering.

She had known, because her mother had told her,

4

how deeply her Uncle had resented the fact that his only sister had run away with his tutor.

He had been at Oxford, and his father, the second Duke, had engaged for him a tutor for the vacations because he was insistent that he should gain his Degree.

Richard Waring was a brilliant, intelligent young man of twenty-nine, who taught the Classics and had successfully coached a number of aristocracy through their finals.

Good-looking, cultured, and coming from respectable stock, he had, however, in the Duke's eyes, been a person of little or no consequence.

His attitude was echoed by his son, Septimus, who was as outraged as his father when it was discovered that Richard Waring had fallen madly in love with his only sister, Lady Elizabeth Bourne.

Richard Waring had approached the Duke in the correct manner, only to be violently abused and shown the front door of the Castle.

That Lady Elizabeth had followed him and that they had run away together had been as startling to her parents as if a bomb had exploded inside the building.

For years Elizabeth was never mentioned.

When Theola was born, four years after their elopement and marriage, Elizabeth wrote to her father and mother telling them that they had a grand-daughter.

The letter was returned unopened.

Only after notification of Elizabeth Waring's death and that of her husband in a train accident did Septimus, who had by then inherited the Dukedom, visit the small cottage outside Oxford where they had lived.

There, he informed a white-faced, unhappy Theola that henceforth she would make her home with him.

Septimus himself had married when he was twenty-one, and had a daughter, Catherine, who was one year older than Theola.

"Do not think I take you under my roof with any pleasure," he had said harshly. "Your father's behaviour was beneath contempt and I shall never forgive him or your mother for the disgrace they brought to our family name."

"Disgrace?" Theola had questioned in surprise. "But what wrong did they do except run away to be married?"

"Do you think it is no disgrace that our blood should be mixed with that of a common parvenu, a man who earned his living by teaching, a man whose forebears doubtless came from the gutter?"

"That is not true!" Theola retorted. "Papa's parents were kind, gentle people, much respected in Bedfordshire, where they lived, and Papa himself was brilliant, as so many—"

She stopped abruptly, as her Uncle slapped her hard across the face.

"How dare you argue with me?" he stormed. "Let me make this quite clear from the very beginning of our acquaintance, Theola. Because you are my niece I cannot allow you to starve. So you will live in my house. But you will obey me and you will not speak of your father and mother to me or to anyone else. Is that understood?"

Theola's cheek was burning, but she did not put her hand up to it.

She only looked at her Uncle, more shocked than frightened by the first violence she had ever encountered in her life.

But she was to learn in the months that followed that her Uncle was ready to strike her whenever she annoyed him, and that was frequently.

He also beat her when she defied him, which was not only an agony which left her weak and fainting, but also a humiliation that left a searing wound upon her mind.

Never had she realised there were people like her Uncle, and indeed her Aunt, in the world.

If her Uncle's blows were painful, her Aunt's slaps and pinches and excessive nagging were almost harder to bear.

Theola had never imagined what it would be like to live with hatred.

Always she had been encircled with love, the love which her mother and father bore for each other and which seemed to glow round them like an aura when they were together.

And the love they had for her always made her feel she was something very precious.

After a few months of what amounted to persecution, she began to creep about the Castle like a little grey ghost, hoping she would remain unnoticed.

She would pray that some magic wand would make her immune to the hard voices that ordered her about and the rough hands which seemed always ready to strike at her when she least expected it.

She tried to be friends with her cousin, Catherine, but found it impossible.

Catherine had a cold nature that she had inherited from both her father and her mother and was indifferent to anything and anyone unless it concerned her personally.

Theola soon found that she was to pay for her board and lodging in her Uncle's house by being a slave to Catherine and becoming more and more her personal servant.

She fetched and carried from the moment she rose in the morning until she went to bed at night.

She mended and pressed Catherine's clothes. She washed most of her fragile garments and had to listen to Catherine's eulogies of herself, knowing she was expected to agree with everything her cousin said and that to argue would be to bring a fierce retribution upon her head.

"I often think I have Greek features," Catherine said once, "and resemble the statues and pictures which are so admired of the Greek goddesses."

With difficulty Theola prevented herself from saying that this was quite untrue.

Catherine was not in the least Greek.

She had the golden hair and blue eyes that were

considered typically English, but her features had nothing particularly to recommend them.

She was spoken of as being beautiful merely because of her social rank and because when she appeared at Balls or parties she was well dressed and carried herself with a kind of insolent pride.

Theola knew more about Greece than about any other part of the world.

It had been her father's love and obsession, and he had talked to Theola of Greek Mythology, shown her pictures of Greek statuary, and fired her with some of his own enthusiasm for the most perfect civilisation the world has ever known.

Richard Waring taught his daughter, as he had taught so many of his students, to love the Classics. He had also said:

"You cannot really understand how a country feels or thinks unless you study its language."

So Theola had learnt French, German, Latin, and Greek, and she had read the great authors aloud to her father. When they discussed them he would listen to her opinions just as he expected her to listen to his.

She had never believed it possible that there were people as important as the Duke of Wellesbourne who never read a book, yet were prepared to lay down the law about every conceivable subject without allowing anyone else to reply.

Sometimes when she went to bed at night at the Castle, so tired that her whole body ached from the tasks which had been set for her during the day, she would think her mind was starving for intelligent conversation.

It was difficult to find time to read.

Lamps illuminated all the rooms in the Castle except for the bed-rooms, which were lit by candles, for economy's sake, and where Theola and the servants were concerned these were strictly limited.

It was therefore impossible to read at night and during the day she had little time.

Theola was reduced to reciting to herself in the darkness the poems and passages of prose she had read with her father.

They moved her because the language was like music and the rhythm of it swept away her unhappiness and lulled her into a dreamless sleep.

And yet, incredibly, after over a year of misery and darkness, here she was in Kavōnia!

It was of course the Duchess, through her Holtz-Melderstein relatives, who had arranged Catherine's marriage with a cousin—King Ferdinand of Kavōnia.

Following the lead of Greece and other European countries that had invited a member of a foreign Royal family to reign over them, the Kavōnians had made Ferdinand their King.

Theola knew they had played with the idea of inviting a King from Scandinavia.

King George of Greece, who was the second son of the heir to the throne of Denmark, had in the ten years he had reigned stabilised the country and brought peace to its people.

But there had been no Danish or Swedish Prince available and they had instead chosen Ferdinand, a relative of the Emperor Franz-Joseph, who had accepted the throne with alacrity.

It was difficult in England to learn very much about him except that he was thirty-five and had already been married, but his wife had died two years earlier, leaving him without an heir.

"I have not seen Ferdinand since he was a little boy," the Duchess said to her daughter, "but in his portraits he appears extremely handsome, very like His Majesty Franz-Joseph when he was young."

She gave a little sigh of satisfaction.

"Protocol in the Royal Palaces in Vienna is strict and very formal. It is, in my opinion, a model for all Royal houses, which I hope, Catherine, you will remember when you are Queen."

"I certainly prefer formality, Mama," Catherine replied. "I have heard of the licence that was tolerated in France under Louis Napoleon. It is not surprising they now have a Republic."

"The less said about the French the better!" the Duchess said reprovingly. "I am sure you will find that King Ferdinand is a very proper and autocratic King."

"I hope so," Catherine replied.

Theola thought it sounded rather frightening.

She had read about the Hapsburgs and she had always thought that in many ways they sounded detestable.

'Surely Kings and Queens should try to understand their people,' she had thought, and knew it was what her father would have expected.

She thought that Catherine would at least try to learn the language of the country over which she was to reign, but when she suggested it, Catherine said sharply:

"King Ferdinand speaks German and English. Why should I wish to learn Kavōnian—a language which is never spoken outside the country?"

"But you will be living in it," Theola said.

"I do not imagine I shall have much contact with the common people," Catherine replied, "and those at Court will certainly speak German or English, as their Monarch does."

Theola thought this was a strange way in which to approach a throne.

At the same time, she was too wise to say so aloud, but she determined that she would learn Kavōnian, which she was certain she would not find difficult, as she already spoke Greek.

She discovered this to be true as soon as she stepped aboard the ship which had been sent by the King to meet them at Marseilles.

They had travelled across France by train in a manner which Theola thought exceedingly luxurious considering the Duke's propensity for not spending money.

There was a Courier to escort them, besides the

Duke's secretary, his valet, a maid for Catherine, and herself.

The Duchess had been declared by her doctors unfit to travel such a long distance.

It had, Theola knew, been a bitter disappointment that she would not see her daughter married.

At the same time, her heart had been troubling her for some years and the Duke was insistent that she should not take any risks.

When they had said good-bye on the steps of the Castle, with the carriage waiting to carry them to the railway-station, Theola thought for the first time since she had known her Aunt that there was a suspicion of tears in her eyes and a softness about her hard features.

"Take care of yourself, my dearest child," she had said to Catherine. "I shall be thinking of you and of course praying for your happiness."

"Good-bye, Mama," Catherine said, her voice devoid of any emotion.

She had stepped into the carriage and Theola was left with her Aunt.

"Good-bye, Aunt Adelaide," she said in her soft voice.

She had curtseyed and wondered if her Aunt was expecting to kiss her, but the Duchess merely looked at her with an unmistakable expression of dislike in her eyes.

"I hope, Theola, you will behave yourself," she said sharply, "and make yourself useful to Catherine."

"Of course, Aunt Adelaide."

"I consider your Uncle has made a great mistake in taking you with him on such an auspicious occasion. I only hope he will not live to regret it."

There was a spiteful note in the Duchess's voice and Theola could do nothing but curtsey again and climb quickly into the carriage to sit with her back to the horses, facing her Uncle and Catherine.

"It is sad for your mother to be left behind," the

11

Duke said to his daughter as the horses started down the drive.

"The journey would have made her ill and that would have been a nuisance," Catherine replied coldly.

"I am sure you are right," the Duke agreed, "but perhaps it would have been wiser to leave Theola with her. She could at least have made herself useful."

Theola had held her breath.

Was it possible that at the last moment she would be sent back to the Castle?

"It is too late now, Papa," Catherine said, "and besides, Theola must make herself useful to me, especially as Emily will go back from Marseilles with the Courier."

"It would be quite useless taking an English servant to a place like Kavōnia," the Duke said, "and, as you say, Theola can do all that is necessary until we can find a Kavōnian servant who will take care of your needs."

The Duke had been right about one thing, Theola found.

Emily, who felt travel-sick in the train, would certainly have been no use on the ship.

Although the Mediterranean was calm when they set sail from Marseilles, they ran into more than one storm before they reached the heel of Italy and turned in to the Adriatic.

Catherine lay in bed groaning and complaining incessantly. It took two stewardesses and Theola all their time to pander to her requirements.

Fortunately, there was a doctor on board who was used to dealing with sea-sick patients. He prescribed sleeping-draughts which gave Catherine long hours of unconsciousness and left Theola free.

There were a number of Kavōnian dignitaries on board representing the King. They were very much to the Duke's liking, as they were ardent card-players.

The gentlemen wiled away the time in the Smoking-Room while Theola, after finding it extremely dull sitting alone in the Salon, soon found a Kavōnian willing to teach her his language.

He was in fact an Aide-de-Camp to the Field-Marshal who led the escorting party, and he might have found time lying heavy on his hands if Theola had not begged him humbly but determinedly to teach her what she wanted to know.

"Why are you so interested, Miss Waring?" he enquired.

"I have longed to visit your country, Captain Petlos," Theola replied.

She thought his eyes lit up at her reply and he answered:

"I hope you will find that it lives up to your expectations."

"I shall certainly appreciate it more if I can talk to your people and understand what they say to me."

When Captain Nichias Petlos found some books in the Library and put paper and pens down on the table in the Salon, she knew that he was not particularly optimistic that she would acquire much knowledge of the Kavōnian language before they reached Port.

But the second day out from Marseilles he exclaimed:

"You are fantastic! I had no idea anyone could learn as quickly as you do!"

"I am only thankful that so many of the words are Greek in origin," Theola said with a smile.

"We are of course a mixture of Greek and Albanian," he said, "and, as you have found, predominantly the former."

By the time they had passed Sicily, Theola was speaking to him with few hesitations and understanding practically everything he said to her.

"You are incredible!" he exclaimed that evening. "I only wish . . ."

He stopped.

"What were you about to say?" Theola asked curiously.

"It is something I had best not say."

13

"Why?"

"Because it might be construed as a criticism."

Theola looked round the empty Salon and smiled.

"Be brave and say it," she suggested. "There is no-one to hear you except some very empty chairs!"

Captain Petlos laughed.

"I was just wishing the King could speak the language of his people."

"He does not do so?" Theola asked incredulously.

Captain Petlos shook his head.

"Unfortunately, no."

"But why? He has been in Kavōnia for ten years. Surely he has been interested enough?"

"I am sure His Majesty has very good reasons for preferring his own language," Captain Petlos said stiffly.

"I am sure he has," Theola agreed. "At the same time, it seems so strange. How do your Kavōnian dignitaries converse with him?"

"They learn to speak German!"

There was a faint smile on Captain Petlos's face, as if some of their efforts had been amusing.

"But surely that is ridiculous!" Theola began, then stopped. "I am sorry . . . I am criticising."

"It is something you must never do when you are in the Palace," Captain Petlos said earnestly. "I am speaking for your own good, Miss Waring. If the King became aware of the conversation we have just had, I assure you I would be demoted to the ranks and you would be sent home."

Theola looked at him wide-eyed.

"Is that true?" she asked after a moment.

"I am warning you because the English are often very outspoken," Captain Petlos said. "It would not be tolerated in Vienna and certainly not in Kavōnia."

"It seems very strange to me," Theola remarked.

"That is why, Miss Waring, I am taking the liberty of telling you to be very careful," Captain Petlos said.

He glanced over his shoulder before he added:

"And incidentally, the Field-Marshal has said that

he considers it very unconventional for us to spend so much time together."

Theola looked at him apprehensively.

"I am sorry if I have got you into trouble."

"It has been a great pleasure," he replied, "and I mean that most sincerely."

He smiled at Theola, and she thought it was the first time since her parents had died that anyone had talked to her as if she was an ordinary human being.

She had been so intent on learning Kavōnian that she had hardly considered the Captain as an individual. He had been there just to teach her and to tell her what she wanted to know.

But now she realised that he was in fact a pleasant young man and, underneath his military exterior, undoubtedly a human one.

She put down her pen and said in Kavōnian:

"Please tell me about your country."

"The truth—or what you can read in a guide-book?" the Captain asked.

"The truth, of course!"

"Kavōnians are happy people if they are not oppressed," he said. "They want to laugh and dance, sing and make love."

There was a pause before he added in a low voice:

"It has not been easy for them to do any of those things for several years."

"Why not?" Theola asked.

"They have had to suffer a great many hardships."

"Why?"

It was obvious that Captain Petlos was choosing his words with care before he said:

"They have been heavily taxed, for one thing."

"But why? What for?"

Captain Petlos shrugged his shoulders.

"Municipal buildings, improvements to the Palace, a large Army."

"I thought you were at peace with the countries round you. Surely you are not threatened by the Turks?"

15

"The Turks have their hands full trying to keep the Albanians under control," Captain Petlos replied. "Whenever Turkey goes to war with a European power, the Albanians seize the opportunity to revolt."

"And the Greeks have no designs on Kavōnia?"

"None at all! King George wants peace."

"Then why such a large Army?"

Again Captain Petlos seemed to be choosing his words carefully.

"There is a certain amount of restlessness in the country."

"Amongst the peasants?"

"They are often hungry, and when there is trouble they take to the mountains."

"But the Army consists of Kavōnians?"

"Nearly all the officers are Austrian."

He saw Theola's look of surprise and added:

"I am one of the exceptions."

"Why?" Theola asked, and thought it sounded rude.

"My father saved the King from an anarchist soon after he came to the throne," Captain Petlos explained. "In return, His Majesty afforded my family special privileges."

He rose as he spoke and began to close the books which they had been reading and picked up the papers. He obviously intended their conversation to come to an end.

"Why did you invite a foreigner to reign over you?" Theola asked. "Surely originally there must have been a Royal Family in Kavōnia?"

"There was a Vasilas on the throne for several centuries," Captain Petlos agreed, "but when the last King died there were many opposing factions and no heir of the right age."

"And is there one now?" Theola asked.

To her surprise, Captain Petlos did not answer her. Instead, he picked up the books and, clicking his heels together as he bowed, said:

"If you will excuse me, Miss Waring, I think the

16

Field-Marshal will be needing me at this hour. It has been an honour to assist you with your studies this afternoon."

He walked across the Salon very stiff and upright in his uniform, and when he was gone Theola gave a little sigh of exasperation.

There was so much she wanted to know, but she thought that if she had to drag every piece of information about Kavōnia out of a reluctant Captain Petlos, there would be little time to learn much before they reached Port.

Nevertheless, in the next two days she did begin to gather a general picture of what was happening in the country.

She thought she might be using her imagination rather freely, but she was sure without Captain Petlos saying so that there was far more unrest in Kavōnia and potential trouble than the Duke had envisaged.

By the time they reached Port she was quite certain that the people were being kept down firmly if not cruelly by their Austrian Overlords.

Actually, she had little time to think about Kavōnia or herself.

The Adriatic was calm and Catherine made an effort to leave her bed and go on deck.

Only Theola could bring her the gown she wanted, could arrange her hair in the manner she fancied, could attend to her while she groaned and muttered at the discomfort of being at sea and her fear of every wave which rocked the ship.

But as they docked, almost on time, there were no waves, the sun was shining, and the sky was a vivid blue.

A brass band on the Quay blared out a noisy welcome, beginning, as Catherine stepped ashore, with the British National Anthem, followed by the Kavōnian.

Nobody paid any attention to Theola and as the Mayor began a formal speech of welcome she had a chance to look round her.

17

She had never imagined that mountains could peak so high or be so exceedingly beautiful against the sky.

The tops were dazzlingly white with snow and below there were pine forests and a profusion of Spanish broom, olives, myrtle, juniper, and bay trees.

Orange and lemon blossom made a fairy-tale background for the wooden houses with their balconies bright with geraniums.

Theola had looked up in one of her father's books the flora and fauna of Northern Greece and knew they would be much the same in Kavōnia.

She was therefore prepared for the beauty of the purple Judas trees, the crimson and white of the rhododendrons, the vivid blue of the gentians, and the pink of the alpine roses.

But as the carriages drove away from Khévea and towards the capital city of Zanthos, never had she imagined she would see such a profusion of flowers in so many different colours.

All along the route there were floral arches, poles decorated with flags, and soldiers guarding the bridges over which they passed.

There were also crowds of sight-seers, peasants in their red skirts and white aprons, their dark hair adorned with flowers, waving and smiling.

It seemed to Theola incredible that Catherine was not more interested in the welcome her future subjects were giving her.

In fact she paid very little attention to the cheers of the people lining the route.

She appeared to have a great deal to say to the Prime Minister, who had met them at the Port as the representative of the King. The Prime Minister had completely ignored Captain Petlos, who sat opposite her, beside Theola.

The Prime Minister was an elderly man with sharp eyes and a guttural voice. Theola realised, to her surprise, that he was Austrian.

The Duke followed in another carriage with the

Field-Marshal and several other dignitaries, all resplendent in uniform or bedecked with gold chains.

There were six carriages in all, besides a number of soldiers on horse-back who rode beside them, with a squadron of Cavaliers leading the procession, while another brought up the rear.

"The soldiers in front belong to His Majesty's personal bodyguard," Captain Petlos told Theola.

"They are very magnificent," she said, thinking that their shining helmets reminded her of those worn by ancient Greek Warriors and wishing once again that her father were there to see them.

There were many Greek physical characteristics, she was sure, amongst the people lining the route, but the procession moved so quickly that they flashed past one group and another took their place before she had time to look closely at them.

It was difficult not to lift her eyes continually towards the heights rising on either side of the road.

'No wonder,' she thought, 'Captain Petlos said that if the people are in trouble, they take to the mountains.'

It would be quite impossible to find a man once he had hidden himself amongst the thick woodlands, the snow-capped peaks, or the deep sharp-cut gorges.

"It is the most exciting country I have ever seen!" Theola told herself.

She wondered why it seemed to arouse no response in Catherine's expression when she looked up from her conversation with the Prime Minister.

Theola would have liked to ask a great many questions of Captain Petlos, but it would have been a breach of etiquette for her to talk unless it was in response to Catherine.

So she remained silent, finding it hard not to wave to the children and not to be disappointed when the small bunches of flowers they threw missed the carriage and fell into the roadway to be trampled under the horses' hoofs.

They must have driven for nearly an hour when Theola realised they were approaching Zanthos and were already passing a few outlying houses.

A few minutes later they crossed a broad river, the bridge guarded by soldiers and garlanded with flowers.

Now they were in narrow streets with humble houses on each side of them which, surprisingly, were undecorated and looked almost as if they were uninhabited.

The shutters were closed and for the first time there were no happy, cheering crowds lining the roadway and no posies being thrown at the carriage.

The horses seemed to move a little quicker and Theola longed to ask Captain Petlos for an explanation of their sombre surroundings.

She had a feeling of oppression, and for the first time since they landed in Kavōnia there was a cloud over the sun.

They passed on through another empty street where there were a few people—very few—and some children, ragged and barefoot, playing by the roadside.

Suddenly the carriage seemed to swerve. There was a scream and the coachman pulled the horses to a standstill.

"What has happened? What has occurred?" the Prime Minister asked sharply.

Captain Petlos opened the door and jumped out.

"We appear to have knocked down a child, Your Excellency," he replied. "She must have run under the wheels."

"A child?" Theola exclaimed.

Without thinking, she moved out swiftly through the door of the carriage, which Captain Petlos had left open, and climbed down onto the roadway.

She saw that a little girl was lying by the front wheel of the carriage and already her bare leg was covered with blood.

Theola hurried forward and knelt down.

After the first scream the child must have been knocked unconscious, for her eyes were closed and she seemed barely to be breathing.

Her leg was pouring blood and Theola thought she must have cut an artery.

She put the child's head in her lap and pulled up her ragged dress.

"Give me your handkerchief, please," she said to Captain Petlos, who was standing beside her.

He started to feel in his pockets and Theola thought perhaps he had not brought one with him.

Impatiently she pulled off the soft silk scarf which she wore round her neck and began to tie it round the little girl's leg above the knee.

"This child must be taken to a hospital at once!" she said. "I am sure she will require medical attention. Is her mother here?"

She looked up and saw, to her astonishment, that the children and the people who had been in the road had disappeared.

There was no-one in sight!

"What is happening?" the Prime Minister asked sharply from the carriage. "We cannot stop here, Captain Petlos."

"A child has been injured, Your Excellency."

"Then leave it to its parents!"

"There is no-one about, Sir."

"Put the child by the roadside. We must drive on."

"We cannot do that!" Theola protested to Captain Petlos. "I have tied a bandage very tightly round the leg to stop the bleeding, but it must be released in not more than ten minutes."

Captain Petlos hesitated and Theola knew he should obey the Prime Minister.

"Call for her parents or a friend. There must be someone about!" she said.

She looked down anxiously at the child's leg. The bleeding was now less intense, but she could see that the wound caused by the wheel had opened the flesh almost to the bone.

"This child must be taken to a hospital!" she said firmly.

"There is no hospital!" Captain Petlos said in a low voice.

Theola looked up at him in astonishment, and as if he felt he must do something he put his hand to his mouth and shouted:

"Will someone come and fetch this child immediately?"

Theola looked up at the shuttered houses but there was no response and she thought for a moment that no-one would come.

Then from one of them a man came walking slowly towards them.

He was tall and broad-shouldered and was wearing a nondescript peasant costume.

"That must be her father," Theola said in relief. "Will you explain to him, in case he does not understand me, that the bandage is to be taken off in ten minutes, otherwise the child may lose her leg, and he must find a doctor quickly!"

The man reached their side.

Then to Theola's utter astonishment she heard the Captain say in a very low voice, hardly above a whisper:

"Are you crazy? If you are recognised you will be shot!"

"I know that!"

The voice was low and deep.

"For God's sake . . ." Captain Petlos murmured.

There was a note of fear in his voice that Theola did not understand.

As if with an effort he said loudly:

"Your child has been most regrettably injured. This lady says the bandage must be released within ten minutes and a doctor must be procured immediately!"

The man did not reply.

He merely bent down to pick up the child who was lying with her head in Theola's lap.

As he did so, Theola looked up at him and for the

first time saw his face. There was no doubt that he was of Greek origin.

Never had she seen a living man who so closely resembled the pictures which her father had shown her.

His features seemed so familiar that she felt as if she knew him.

Then as their eyes met she saw an expression in his that made her feel almost as if he had struck her.

She would never have believed that any human being could have looked at her with such contempt.

"Who is that man?"

The Prime Minister asked the question sharply.

Captain Petlos stepped back to the side of the carriage.

"I think he is the father of the child, Your Excellency."

The man who was now holding the child said to Theola quietly:

"Thank you for your assistance—but may I ask a favour?"

"What is it?" Theola enquired.

"Will you help me carry the child carefully back to the house? If you will hold one side of her, I will hold the other. It will be easier for her."

"Of course," Theola agreed.

She could not help thinking, however, that it would be quite simple for such a tall, strong man to carry the little girl by himself.

But because she realised how bad the child's leg was, she was prepared to agree to anything which might alleviate her suffering.

They moved side by side up the short incline towards the houses, carrying the unconscious child between them, and only as they actually reached the door did an unseen hand open it from the inside.

Suddenly Theola realised that the way she was walking created a screen between the Prime Minister and the man on the other side of the child.

They stepped into the house.

Theola had a quick glimpse of a poor room, al-

23

most bare of furniture, in which there were two people, an elderly man sitting in a chair and a woman
with tears streaming down her face who was obviously the child's mother.

She moved towards them, her arms outstretched,
and even as she did so, behind her Theola heard the
Prime Minister shout:

"It is Alexius Vasilas! Shoot him! Shoot him—you
fools!"

Almost without haste, the man who had been carrying the child put her into the mother's arms, then
without a word moved across the room and out
through another door.

It closed behind him just as Captain Petlos, pistol
in hand, and four soldiers came hurrying from the carriages up to the front door.

Theola was not quite certain why she did it, but
deliberately she turned to stand in the narrow doorway, blocking it completely.

"What is it? What is happening?" she asked.

"Let me pass, Miss Waring," Captain Petlos replied. "I have my orders."

"What orders?" she enquired.

"The man who was helping you with the child is to
be detained."

Theola did not move.

"I thought your orders were to shoot him, Captain!"

"I have to find him, Miss Waring."

"I think he has gone for a doctor," Theola said, "and
it would be a great mistake to delay him. The
child's leg, as you well know, is badly injured."

"I must do my duty," the Captain replied.

However, it was impossible for him to enter the
house without pushing Theola out of the way.

Two of the soldiers with him went to the house next
door, tried the door, which was obviously locked, and
hammered on it without response.

Theola made no effort to move.

"Come back! Come back!" she heard the Prime
Minister order.

Now a Senior Officer from one of the other carriages said sharply:

"The procession should proceed, Your Excellency. It is not safe to remain here."

"Then proceed—proceed at once!" the Prime Minister said testily. "As usual, Vasilas has evaded us. Why did no-one inform me that he was in the city?"

There was no answer to this, but Theola realised that the danger was past.

She turned back to say to the woman with the child:

"Please . . . have your daughter's leg seen to immediately, and undo the bandage round her leg . . . in six or seven minutes."

She spoke in her halting Kavōnian but the woman seemed to understand.

She nodded her head.

Theola was carrying a reticule suspended from her wrist. She opened it and taking out a gold sovereign set it down on a chair that was near the door.

"For the little girl," she said softly.

Then she followed Captain Petlos back to the carriage.

"Really, Theola!" Catherine exclaimed as she climbed in. "How could you do anything so irresponsible, so completely ridiculous, as to mess about with that child? This is a dangerous part of the city and we should not be stopping here."

There were a great many things that Theola could have replied, but she felt it would be useless to say them.

"I am sorry, Catherine," she said humbly.

"And so you should be," Catherine answered sharply. "I am sure Papa will be extremely annoyed when he hears of your behaviour."

She paused to add spitefully:

"You have blood on your gown and you look a complete mess!"

Theola looked down at her skirt and saw that Catherine was right.

There was a large streak of crimson blood near the hem.

'The first blood I have seen shed in Kavōnia!' she thought unhappily.

CHAPTER TWO

The carriage started off and Catherine turned to the Prime Minister.

"Who is this man Vasilas?" she enquired curiously.

"He is a revolutionary," the Prime Minister replied, "a man who stirs up trouble wherever he goes. The troops have my instructions to shoot him on sight, but some are so stupid they appear not to recognise him."

He glared at Captain Petlos as he spoke. Then, obviously feeling it would be undignified to rebuke him in front of strangers, he said in a more genial tone:

"But you need not be afraid, Lady Catherine. I assure you that as soon as we arrive at the Palace the Field-Marshal will order the man to be found, wherever he is hiding. Then we shall hear no more of him."

Theola glanced from under her eye-lashes at Captain Petlos. She could see he was looking very pale and she sensed that he was afraid.

She could not understand exactly what was going on, but she felt that it was of significance.

If Alexius Vasilas was in fact a member of the family that had previously reigned in Kavōnia, why was he dressed as a peasant? And why was he apparently living in the slum through which they had just passed?

It was obvious from what the Prime Minister said that they had been trying to kill or capture him for some time. Under those circumstances, it seemed extraordinary that he should have been brave enough to go to the assistance of the injured child.

It was all very perplexing. At the same time, it was intriguing! There was another thing that needed to be explained.

Why had the poor parts of the city been so quiet and the streets deserted?

Once the procession was clear of them, there were again arches of flowers, flags waving, and crowds cheering.

And now Catherine's picture appeared everywhere —on hoardings, on the fronts of houses, hanging from the lamp-standards, and the people held up roughly printed paper reproductions.

Catherine looked at the throngs of cheering citizens and now seemed pleased.

"They all have my picture!" she exclaimed to the Prime Minister.

"They treasure it, Lady Catherine," he replied. "And they welcome you as their future Queen, not only because you are English and very beautiful, but also because of the legend."

"What legend?" Catherine asked.

"There is an ancient prophecy that when a fair-haired, white-skinned Princess comes from over the sea to rule in Kavōnia, the country will enjoy peace and great prosperity."

"How interesting," Catherine remarked.

"As soon as I saw your portrait, Lady Catherine," the Prime Minister said, "I knew you were the Princess of the legend."

"But I am not a Princess," Catherine said almost reluctantly.

"That is a rough translation of the Kavōnian word which means 'lovely lady of great importance.'"

Cathering smiled with pleasure, but Theola, hearing the story, was certain that it was the Prime Minister who had whipped up the crowd's enthusiasm by publicising the old prophecy.

'Perhaps,' she thought, 'if he had not done so, Catherine would have arrived to find empty streets and closed shutters.'

Then she told herself that she was being too imaginative.

Of course the Kavōnians would want their King to marry and would be prepared to celebrate the event.

Catherine was smiling and waving while looking very English and very attractive in her pale-blue gown which matched the colour of her eyes, and with the feathers on her bonnet moving in the breeze.

They passed through a large Square and several broad streets with fine houses standing in large gardens. Then ahead they saw the Palace.

It was extremely impressive and as they drew nearer Theola realised that it was in fact a replica of the Schönbrunn in Vienna.

There were fountains playing and statues to decorate the wide Court-Yard in front of it. The soldiers on guard were as colourful as the great company of distinguished guests who were waiting on the steps of the Palace itself.

The women's jewellery and the decorations of the men glittered in the sunshine which seemed to envelop everything as if it were a blessing from Heaven itself.

As the carriage came to a stop, Theola could see advancing towards them down a red carpet a figure wearing a white uniform who she knew must be the King.

It was all very dramatic and she wondered if Catherine's heart was beating wildly at the thought of meeting her future husband.

As the King came nearer, Theola was disappointed.

Up to now everything had seemed part of a fairy-story and so romantic that she had expected the King to be tall and handsome, perhaps with Greek features like Alexius Vasilas.

Then she remembered that the King was a Haps-burg; he was, in fact, not the Prince Charming she had hoped to see, but a rather ordinary-looking man, not very tall, slightly corpulent, and having a proud, cold, and aloof manner not unlike Catherine's.

'Perhaps they are well suited to each other,' Theola thought.

Following Catherine from the carriage, she sank down in a deep curtsey.

There was so much to look at, so much to interest her, that it was not until two hours later that Theola had time to think of herself and remember that her gown was stained with blood.

She had been introduced to an enormous number of people, all of whom spoke German and were in fact, Theola was sure, Austrian by birth.

Now that she thought about it, it was impossible to remember if she had met a single Kavōnian amongst those to whom she had spoken.

She could not help feeling that she and Catherine were rather like strange animals in a Zoo, as the eyes of everyone present were upon them and their most commonplace remarks were received with rapt attention.

'Catherine will love feeling so important,' she thought.

There was no doubt that her cousin seemed to be enjoying herself for the first time since they had left England.

Even the Duke had been flattered into an affability which was rare for him.

When finally Catherine was alone with Theola in the magnificent white-and-gold Sitting-Room that was part of the Queen's Apartments, she exclaimed with a note of elation in her voice:

"Mama was right! I shall enjoy being a Queen!"

"I thought you would," Theola said, "and the people were really pleased to see you."

"Of course they were!" Catherine remarked. "The Prime Minister told me over and over again how delighted he and his colleagues were for an English-woman to grace the throne."

"I was thinking of the Kavōnians," Theola said.

"Oh—them!" Catherine remarked. "They will doubtless enjoy the wedding-festivities which the King assures me will be very extensive."

"Do you realise there is no hospital in Zanthos?" Theola asked.

"That is not my concern!" Catherine snapped. "And if you are still thinking of that child over whom you behaved so disgracefully, Theola, you can just forget her!"

Theola did not answer, and after a moment Catherine went on:

"If that is typical of the manner in which you intend to behave in a foreign country, I shall ask Papa to take you back to England with him. I may do so anyway. I am sure there are many charming and delightful Austrian ladies here who would be only too pleased to act as my Ladies-in-Waiting."

Theola drew in her breath.

She knew only too well what sort of life she would find waiting for her at home, and she had never thought that, having reached Kavōnia, Catherine might be ready to dispense with her services so quickly.

"I am . . . sorry," she said humbly.

"And so you should be!" Catherine declared. "But

31

kindly behave yourself in the future, Theola. I could
see that the Prime Minister was annoyed at the manner in which you prevented them from shooting that
rebel."

With difficulty Theola bit back the words which
came to her lips and instead asked meekly:

"May I go to my room, Catherine, and change my
gown? You will need me in attendance, I think, in an
hour's time, when we are to meet the King for a Reception."

"Yes, and hurry," Catherine answered. "I shall want
you to explain to the new maids the right way to
dress me, and you must see to my hair."

"Yes, of course," Theola answered.

A maid showed her to her room, which was next to
the enormous and extremely impressive bed-room
occupied by Catherine.

The Queen's Room was beautiful and the furnish-
ings had obviously been brought to Kavōnia from
Vienna. There was no mistaking its baroque style,
the glittering silver-framed mirrors, and the large,
richly inlaid cupboard and chests.

Instead of fireplaces, the rooms in the Palace were
heated by tiled stoves of ceramic-work copied from
the Palace in Vienna.

In the Sitting-Room and passages the pictures
which decorated the walls were all of the King's
Hapsburg ancestors or views of Austria.

Theola was sure that if Kavōnia had any culture
of its own, it would certainly not be in evidence in the
Palace.

Her own bed-room was of course much smaller
than Catherine's, but was comfortable and, again,
very Viennese in style.

There were two maids busily unpacking Theola's
trunks as she entered, and when she thanked them in
Kavōnian they were obviously delighted and looked
at her with smiling faces.

One of them was very young, while the other, who
was obviously training her, was an older woman.

"You speak our language, *Fraulein?*" she exclaimed in delight.

"I am trying to speak it," Theola replied, "and you must help me, because I have not been learning it for very long."

"In the Palace we have to speak only German, *Fraulein,*" the maid said.

"Not when you are with me," Theola answered. "It would help me if you would talk to me in Kavōnian, as that would be the easiest way for me to learn the language."

Both the maids were delighted at the suggestion. Meanwhile, Theola knew how angry Catherine would be if she took too long in changing her gown.

It was not difficult for her to choose what she would wear.

The Duchess had, as usual, been extremely mean when it came to expending money on clothes for her niece.

"No-one will look at you, Theola," she had said, "and the less conspicuous you make yourself, the better!"

She had therefore chosen the cheapest materials in plain drab colours which made Theola's heart sink every time she looked at them.

Although she and her mother had little money to spend, they had made their own gowns in soft, pastel colours which her father always admired and which Theola had known were particularly becoming to her.

She was the same height as Catherine, but she was much slighter, principally because she was worked so hard, and she also had much more delicate features.

Once when Theola was a child she had said to her father:

"I wish I looked like a Greek goddess, Papa! Then you would love me as much as you love the statues of Aphrodite."

Richard Waring had laughed.

"I love you much more than any goddess made of marble or painted on canvas."

He put his arms round his daughter, looked down at her face, and said:

"Perhaps you will never look like the Greek Aphrodite, my darling, but many men, I am quite sure, will find you have exactly the same effect on their hearts."

"But I want to look Greek," Theola insisted.

"That is what you do look," Richard Waring said, "but not like a goddess living on Mount Olympus, but rather one of the nymphs who inhabited the island of Delos and came from the sea to serve the god of light."

"Tell me about them! Tell me!" Theola begged.

Her father had related how in the ninth century B.C. there had been rumours of a young and handsome God armed with a bow of gold who had been born on the island of Delos and had consecrated it with his presence.

"Who was the God?" Theola enquired.

"He was called Apollo," her father answered, "and when I visited Delos I found that the air was still a 'dancing, quivering flame.'"

"I do not understand," Theola said.

"It is difficult to explain," Richard Waring answered, "but where the gods lived, especially Apollo, there is a special light, strange, glittering, and shining in the air, a mysterious quivering, the beating of silver wings, and the whirling of silver wheels."

Richard Waring had spoken almost as if he was in a trance, and Theola had listened, not understanding, but loving the music of his voice, knowing that his memories moved him with a strange magic.

"And always where there were the gods," her father continued, "there were nymphs beside the streams in the mists which covered the Greek islands in the early morning and in the foam of the sea."

He sighed before he went on:

"Apollo conquered the world by the power of his beauty. He had no earthly resources, no Army, no Navy, no powerful Government, but he brought sun-

light to the human mind and they worshipped him
as he leapt forth into the light of day."

Richard Waring could make everything he spoke of
sound real, because he himself believed in it, and to
Theola he opened a world of beauty of which she became a part.

From that moment she too worshipped Apollo and
to her he personified love . . . a love which as she
grew older she thought she would find with a man.

As the years passed she began to understand why
her father had thought she resembled one of the
Greek nymphs.

She had a very sensitive, heart-shaped face in which
the predominant feature was her large eyes.

Her eyes, although she did not realise it, held a
mystery in their depths, almost as if she were looking
into the unseen world with which her father was so
familiar.

Her hair was fair, but not the gold of Catherine's.
In fact it was so pale as to seem almost colourless, and
yet there were lights in it which made it at times
seem alive.

Her skin was very white, and the dark, sombre
colours in which her Aunt dressed her made her appear unnaturally pale.

Sometimes Theola wondered if the Duchess deliberately tried to extinguish in her the light of which
her father had spoken and which she knew existed in
her soul.

Living in the Castle, harshly treated, constantly
abused and physically assaulted, made it hard to remember the days when she had felt as if she danced
on air and was part of the beauty which her father
seemed always to carry with him.

It was difficult when she was continually hurrying
from place to place, obeying order after order, to re-
call all he had taught her.

Only when she was alone in the darkness at night
would she remember that he had said:

"In the silence can be heard the voice of the God calling on men to seek in themselves the lucidity of the Holy Light."

"Which gown will you wear, *Fraulein?*" the elder maid asked, interrupting Theola's thoughts.

She resisted an impulse to retort that it did not matter, they were all so ugly that no-one would notice her anyway.

Hanging in the wardrobe, they seemed incongruous when she thought of the sunshine that existed outside, the dazzling snow on the peaks of the mountains, and the flowers which she was sure when she had time to examine them would make Kavōnia seem an earthly Paradise.

Catherine would be wearing to the Reception a white gown trimmed with small pink roses and ornamented with blue ribbons.

It was a gown that had been especially designed to frame her pink-and-white beauty and golden hair so that she would look the living embodiment of every woman's picture of the ideal bride.

For Theola there was a choice between grey batiste of the cheapest quality, a dark-brown merino, and an ugly, dull-blue polonaise which reminded her of the sky in winter.

"I will wear the grey," she said automatically.

As the maids helped her into it she tidied her hair, hardly bothering to look at herself in the mirror as she did so.

Quick as she was in returning to Catherine's room, she was not quick enough and her cousin was already incensed.

"Tell these idiots to find my best silk stockings!" she said angrily as Theola came into the room.

She spoke in English and although the maids did not understand what she was saying, there was no mistaking the exasperation in her voice. Theola saw that the women looked worried and apprehensive.

She was sure they were only too anxious to please,

but Catherine was as usual impatient, and expected a servant to know automatically what she wanted. She did not even trouble to explain her needs clearly.

Theola quickly found the stockings and told the maids in their own language how their new Mistress wished to be waited on.

Soon they were smiling and hurrying to obey her instructions while Catherine, regarding her own reflection in the mirror, became better-tempered.

"This gown is certainly becoming," she said. "I cannot believe it will be equalled by any other woman in the Palace."

"You will outshine them all," Theola said and meant it.

"That is what I mean to do," Catherine said, "and I intend to have all my gowns in the future ordered from Paris."

"That could prove very expensive," Theola said.

Catherine shrugged her shoulders.

"The money will be found—you may be certain of that!" she said. "Although the Prime Minister was telling me that they have a large national debt ..."

"I hope not!" Theola said quickly.

Catherine looked at her in surprise.

"Why should it trouble you?" she asked. "It certainly does not concern me!"

"It will mean more taxes on the people," Theola answered. "You can imagine how much they have had to pay already to build this huge Palace."

"And why not?" Catherine enquired. "They could hardly expect their King to live in a mud hut!"

There was an aggressive note in her voice.

With difficulty Theola prevented herself from saying that such vast extravagance seemed incompatible with the fact that apparently they could not afford a hospital.

But she knew there was no point in saying such things to Catherine, for she was concerned only with herself and her own appearance.

Theola could not help remembering the poverty of the room in the house into which she had carried the injured child.

The floor had been bare and there had been no luxuries of any sort. Two hard wooden chairs, a deal-table, and a bed in one corner comprised the only furniture, and she had known by the appearance of both the mother and the child that they were under-nourished.

She could understand only too well why there was what Captain Petlos had called "restlessness" amongst the Kavōnians.

Was it surprising, when their King expended enor-mous sums on his Palace and apparently little or nothing was done for the poorest of his subjects?

She found herself praying that the soldiers, who by now had been sent in search of Alexius Vasilas, would not find him.

He had looked at her with contempt because, she knew, he considered her a part of the Régime against which he was rebelling.

But he was in fact the most handsome man she had ever seen.

He might have been the model for Apollo himself as her father had described him.

"Nothing the Greeks ever created," Richard War-ing had said once, "was as magnificent as this youth who tore the darkness from the human soul and let in Divine light."

'Is that what Alexius Vasilas is trying to do for the people of Kavōnia?' Theola wondered, and then told herself that she was just being imaginative.

Perhaps he was nothing more than an anarchist who hated law and order and wished to create chaos without having anything to put in its place.

Then she told herself that no-one could be so hand-some or have the look of Apollo and not be one with those who brought to the world "the glory of the gods."

'One day perhaps he will succeed in all he wishes to do,' Theola thought, and found herself wondering if she would ever see him again.

It certainly seemed unlikely, for when she later moved among the company of dignitaries of all sorts and kinds she found that they all were Austrian.

"Have you lived here long?" she asked one lady.

"I came to Kavōnia ten years ago," she answered. "His Majesty wishes to be surrounded by his own countrymen."

"And you did not mind leaving Austria?" Theola enquired.

"Sometimes I used to feel home-sick," the lady replied, "but now there are so many of us here and a great number are related in one way or another. Kavōnia has a delightful climate. That, as I have often said to my husband, is its one great asset!"

Theola gathered that there were Balls which took place once or twice a week, given either by the King or by members of the Court circle.

There was a Theatre where plays were performed by a resident cast, while occasionally foreign actors visited Zanthos from Greece or Italy.

"We are a very gay little community," a Gentleman-in-Waiting said to Theola later in the evening, "and I am sure, Miss Waring, you will find a great deal to amuse you."

"I hope to have the opportunity of exploring the whole country," Theola replied.

The Gentleman-in-Waiting looked at her in surprise.

"Everything of any importance takes part in the capital," he answered. "Of course there is wild-boar hunting, although I doubt if you would enjoy that, and we shoot roe-deer and chamois at the right time of the year. But for the ladies there is plenty to do at Court and I can assure you, Miss Waring, new faces as pretty as yours, and of course our future Queen's, are very much appreciated."

There were a number of young Austrain bachelors who Theola learnt were all officers in the Army, but she found them stiff and difficult to talk to.

She guessed that while they accorded her a certain amount of respect because she was the Duke's niece and Catherine's cousin, they were not particularly impressed by her appearance or the manner in which she was treated by her relatives.

She was therefore convinced that she would soon be written off in their estimation as a person of no importance.

It was a prophecy that was to be fulfilled.

Catherine's sharp admonitions to Theola and the Duke's almost-insulting rebukes in public were soon noted by the snobby and class-conscious Austrians.

They were famous in Vienna for their love of protocol, which was so excessive that they could hardly raise a glass to their lips without the danger of infringing upon some peculiar rule of etiquette.

"I am told," Catherine said to Theola, "that in Vienna it is correct for ladies to wear gloves even when they are eating their meals."

"How ridiculous!" Theola exclaimed. "I cannot imagine anything more uncomfortable! It must have been invented by a Queen with ugly hands!"

"That is the remark, I am told, that the Empress Elizabeth made," Catherine said, "and shocked the whole Court!"

"Well, I hope you are not going to suggest such an innovation here," Theola said. "I am sure no-one would appreciate it in this heat."

"I might consider it," Catherine answered loftily.

Every day, Theola noticed, she became more and more regal and she knew this was because Catherine was taking her cue from the King.

Every time she met His Majesty, Theola found him a pompous bore and incredibly self-opinionated.

There were moments when she realised, not without amusement, that the Duke was finding it extremely hard to tolerate the manner in which his future son-in-law condescended to him and completely ignored his remarks, as if they were of no importance.

It was obvious that the Courtiers were all frightened of King Ferdinand, and Theola was certain that he was extremely ruthless in Government.

It was easy to see from the manner in which he treated the servants and the junior officials who came in contact with him that he was an autocrat who thought of no-one's feelings except his own.

Theola would have been sorry for Catherine if she had not realised that her cousin actually found King Ferdinand's behaviour admirable in every possible way and was determined to emulate him.

When Theola came into the bed-room she often found the maids in tears, and although she never actually saw her do so, she suspected that Catherine hit them with her hair-brush or anything else that was available, just as the Duchess had hit Theola when she was at the Castle.

Because Catherine was far too impatient to teach her maid-servants anything, she expected Theola to be in attendance on her at every possible moment.

If Theola had had little time to herself at the Castle, she had still less time at the Palace.

At the same time, she was sure that it was very unlikely that after the wedding she would be sent back to England with the Duke.

She could not imagine that Catherine would be able to manage without her, and that in itself was a relief.

But Theola began to fear that she would never have a chance to see anything but the exquisite stucco rooms of the Palace and the formal gardens which surrounded it.

"Do we never drive in the city or outside Zanthos?" she asked Captain Petlos.

"Very seldom," he answered, "and not at this time of the year. The ladies consider it too hot."

"I would like to ride over the countryside," Theola said with a smile.

"Perhaps you will have a chance after the wedding," the Captain replied. "But if you suggest it now, it will cause a lot of adverse comment, because no-one else rides."

Theola sighed, then she said:

"I sound very spoilt, but I feel confined because we never leave the Palace."

"I often feel like that myself," Captain Petlos answered. "But I do get away when the Field-Marshal inspects the troops in other parts of the country."

"There is so much I want to see," Theola said wistfully.

She was thinking of the mountains and the flowers, the valleys and the great forests in which she learnt there were brown bears, lynx, and wild cats.

"You will have to persuade your cousin, when she is Queen, to go on picnics and even expeditions," Captain Petlos suggested.

Theola was sure that he was well aware that Catherine would wish to do nothing of the sort.

She would be completely content reigning over the small Court and being amused by the intrigues, the gossip, and the artificial amusements that took place day after day.

"It is wrong of me to complain," Theola told herself, "when I am so lucky to be here at all, and so relieved to be away from the Castle."

She had seen little of her Uncle because there were so many gentlemen wishing to entertain him. But two days before the wedding he sent for her.

She went into the Queen's Sitting-Room, where he was waiting, feeling suddenly apprehensive in case he should have decided to take her home with him.

"I want to talk to you, Theola," he said as she entered the room nervously.

"Yes, Uncle Septimus?"

"I shall be leaving here the day after the wedding," he said, "and as Catherine is keeping you busy I may not have a chance to talk to you again before I go."

"No, Uncle Septimus."

This did not sound as if he intended to take her with him, and Theola waited, her fear of what he was about to say subsiding a little.

"You will stay in Kavōnia until you are no longer of any use to Catherine," the Duke said, "but I want to make one thing quite clear."

"What is that, Uncle Septimus?"

"You will behave yourself with great propriety, and you will not at any time be interested in any man, or permit him to be interested in you."

Theola looked at him with wide eyes.

"I do not . . . understand."

"Then let me make it quite clear," the Duke said. "Whether you are living in England or Kavōnia, you are still under my guardianship and you cannot marry, Theola, without my consent. That I do not intend to give!"

"While I am . . . here, Uncle Septimus?"

"Wherever you are," the Duke replied. "As I have told you before, your mother brought disgrace to our name."

Theola did not speak and he continued more forcefully:

"I do not intend to have to explain to any man who may wish you to be his wife that my sister—my only sister—with the noble blood of generations in her veins, disgraced herself by marrying beneath her, marrying a man who was little more than a servant!"

The disgust in the Duke's voice was even harder to bear than were his words. Theola clenched her hands together to prevent herself from defending her father.

"Here they have accepted you as my niece and Catherine's cousin," the Duke went on, "and there is no reason for anyone to know of your mother's appalling *mésalliance*."

He paused before he said forcefully:

"But you know of it—and so do I. That is why you will remain a spinster, Theola, expurgating the sins

43

of your parents by service and humility until you die!"

"U-Uncle . . . Septimus . . ." Theola began, only to be silenced as the Duke roared at her:

"Do not dare to argue with me! There is nothing further to be said on the matter, save that you will behave yourself and do as I have told you. One suggestion of improper behaviour and Catherine has my orders to send you back home immediately!"

He paused before he added:

"There you will be punished in a manner which will make you sorry that you ever disobeyed me! Do you understand?"

"I . . . understand . . . Uncle Septimus."

"Then that is all I have to say to you," the Duke said. "You are extremely fortunate in that Catherine finds you useful. Otherwise you would not be here at this moment, and I should not leave without you. You can show your gratitude in a practical manner, and be certain you do so!"

The Duke turned as he finished speaking and walked from the Queen's Sitting-Room.

He closed the door behind him and Theola was alone. She put her hands up to her face.

She could not believe that what he had said could be the truth; that she was never to be married, never to know the joy and happiness her father and mother had found together.

It seemed to her impossible that he could not understand what an exceptional person her father had been.

Everyone at Oxford had proclaimed Richard Waring's brilliance. He had been elected a Fellow of his College and there was no-one in the University who did not both respect and admire him for his learning and like him for himself.

When he died, Theola received hundreds of letters of condolence and appreciation of his great qualities, which she had never dared to show her Uncle.

She was sure he would refuse to read them and

would doubtless deprive her of the pleasure of keeping them.

Everything that she had owned in her home and which she had believed to be hers had, on the death of her father and mother, been either sold or thrown away.

The Duke had not permitted her to bring to the Castle anything but her own personal clothing, and furthermore, the money her parents had left, although it was only a small amount, had been confiscated.

When they were preparing to leave for Kavōnia she had said to her Uncle:

"Will you give me some money, Uncle Septimus? I feel I shall need a little for my personal requirements."

"And what might they be?" the Duke had asked in a hostile voice.

"I . . . I might wish to buy a few . . . articles of clothing from time to time," Theola answered, "or to tip the servants."

"As you will be little more than a servant yourself, they will not expect it," the Duke said, "and as for clothing—Catherine will doubtless provide you with what you would require."

"I cannot go with nothing in my purse," Theola had protested.

"In which case I suggest you leave your purse behind!" the Duke had retorted.

It was an humiliating position in which to be, Theola thought, and the only consolation was that she had three precious gold sovereigns hidden away in a trinket-box.

Her father had given them to her on one of her birthdays because each one of them commemorated an important moment in her life.

One was dated 1855—the year she was born. Another was minted in 1868, the year in which she had been confirmed, and the third, the year in which he had given her all three, was when she was fifteen.

"When you have enough, dearest," her mother had said, "we will make them into a bracelet."

"That will be fun, Mama," Theola replied.

But there had been no more sovereigns, and now they were literally the only money she possessed.

She thought she would never spend them except in an emergency.

Yet impulsively, because she had been so distressed at the child's injuries when they had entered the city, she had left one of her precious sovereigns in the poverty-stricken house.

She had not regretted it. At the same time, she wondered what would happen when she was forced to ask Catherine for a new gown, knowing that her cousin was as mean and ungenerous as the Duke and Duchess.

'Perhaps she will give me one of her old ones,' Theola thought hopefully.

She wondered what it would be like to wear the beautiful, elaborate, elegant dresses with their long trains with which Catherine had clearly startled the ladies at Court.

The crinoline had gone out of fashion five years earlier; now the gowns were swept back over a bustle to fall behind the wearer in a cascade of frills, bows, loops, and fringes which flowed into an elegant train.

Shoulders were bare in the evening and tight bodices were moulded to the figure, and Theola often thought that her father would have admired the almost-Grecian manner in which the breasts and the small waist of a woman were revealed.

But her own gowns, on the Duchess's instructions, fitted loosely and had no trains.

The very severity of them, because trimmings were expensive, made Theola feel that her appearance, as her Aunt had obviously intended, was humble and subservient.

'If only there were a fairy to wave a magic wand over me,' she thought as she dressed for dinner, 'and give me a gown that encircled my shoulders like a cloud and billowed out behind me like a white-crested wave.'

But instead she knew she looked like a dark shadow in her sombre gown as she followed the resplendent Catherine, blazing with jewels with which the King had presented her, into the Salon.

"Only two more days!" Catherine said as they went upstairs after an evening in which there had been a theatrical performance followed by dancing.

"You are looking forward to your wedding?" Theola asked.

"I shall be a Queen!" Catherine replied.

"And you will be happy with . . . King Ferdinand?"

Theola asked the question hesitatingly, hoping Catherine would not think it an impertinence.

"I find him pleasant to be with," Catherine said after a moment.

There was a pause, as if she considered her words.

"And I admire the manner in which he is governing this country."

"He has talked to you about it?" Theola asked.

"He has told me the people need a firm hand and must be kept under control," Catherine said. "They are partly Greek and therefore emotionally excitable!"

She spoke scathingly and Theola said without thinking:

"It is their country!"

"On the contrary," Catherine replied, "it is Ferdinand's, and he has told me how much he has done already to improve the international status of Kavōnia."

"In what way?" Theola asked.

"Other Monarchs regard him with respect. After all, he has reigned for twelve years, and look what he has done in such a short time."

"What has he . . . done?" Theola asked cautiously.

"You have seen the Palace?" Catherine asked. "It was a very unimportant, crumbling building when he arrived, and the city itself was just a jumble of poor houses without a decent shop. Why, the ladies even had to send to Naples or Athens if they required lace or ribbons!"

Theola said nothing.

There was in fact, she thought, nothing to say.

Catherine would not be interested in the feelings or indeed the sufferings of the Kavōnians, and after all, she herself knew very little about them.

The poverty-stricken room she had seen in the suburbs of Zanthos, and what she had heard of the restlessness of the peasants outside the city, constituted her entire knowledge of the situation.

"I must go to bed," Catherine said. "I do not wish to be tired tomorrow when we will be receiving a number of guests who will be arriving for the wedding the next day."

"You do not feel at all nervous?" Theola asked.

"Why should I?" Catherine replied. "After all, as you well know, Theola, I am well fitted to be a Queen, and I shall make a beautiful bride."

"Of course," Theola agreed.

"The Cathedral is not very large," Catherine went on, "but I expect everyone will be squeezed in somehow."

"Surely the national religion of Kavōnia is Greek Orthodox?" Theola asked in a puzzled voice.

"I believe so," Catherine replied indifferently, "but the King is a Catholic. Nevertheless, he has decided to be married in the Greek Cathedral. It is far more impressive than the Catholic Church, which is very small."

"Can he do that?" Theola enquired.

"Ferdinand can do anything!" Catherine replied proudly. "Of course the stupid old Archbishop has refused to participate in the ceremony as he was expected to do, and he has retired in a huff to his Monastery in the mountains!"

She laughed scornfully.

"I can imagine that the performance of a Catholic

marriage in a Greek Orthodox Cathedral would cause
great resentment among the Kavōnians," Theola said
quietly.

"Who cares?" Catherine asked. "I shall be married,
whoever leads the Service, and then I shall be
crowned Queen."

Theola said nothing. She was sure that if the King
took over the Cathedral for his wedding and introduced the Priests of another Church, it would be considered an unprecedented insult.

Catherine moved across the room towards the bed-
room where her maids were waiting to help her undress.

"As soon as I am married," she said, "I intend to
change the colour of the curtains in this room. I do not
think pink is really becoming to me. Blue would be
much more effective, and the sofas too are not as comfortable as I should like."

"Surely it would be very expensive to redo the
whole room?" Theola suggested.

"What does expense matter?" Catherine enquired.
"The materials can come from Vienna or Paris, and
I have an idea that I would like a chandelier of Vene-
tian glass."

She waited for Theola to open the bed-room door
for her and as she did so the door of the Sitting-Room
was suddenly flung open.

Both the girls turned to see the Duke standing in
the doorway.

Wearing his evening clothes, his coat bestrewn with
decorations and the blue Order of the Garter across
his chest, the expression on his face made Theola draw
in her breath.

"Quick, Catherine!" he exclaimed. "Change into
your riding-habit. We are leaving immediately!"

"Leaving, Papa? What do you mean?"

"You and the King are being taken to a place of
safety," the Duke said. "There is no time to be lost!"

"But why?" Catherine cried. "And why should we
not be safe here?"

"Because a revolution has broken out," the Duke replied. "The Prime Minister believes it is nothing that will be settled in a day or so. The Government cannot risk either the King or yourself being in danger."

"Papa! Papa!" Catherine cried, her composure crumbling, an expression of fear contorting her face.

"Do as I say, Catherine!" her father thundered. "Change into your riding-clothes and be ready to leave within five minutes."

Catherine gave a little cry of horror. Then as the Duke turned to leave the room Theola asked:

"Am I to go with Catherine, Uncle Septimus?"

He looked back at her over his shoulder.

"You are in no danger as a British subject," he said indifferently. "You stay here! I will tell someone to look after you."

CHAPTER THREE

Screaming with impatience, Catherine pulled off the long gloves she was wearing and threw them to the floor.

"Quickly, Theola! Undo my gown . . . hurry, you idiot!"

There was no sign of any maids, and, having helped Catherine undress, Theola ran to the wardrobe to find her riding-habit.

The first one she took out was rose-pink and Catherine yelled at her:

"Not that colour, you fool! I should be inconspicuous. I might be shot! Give me something dark!"

Hastily Theola lifted down a habit of sapphire-blue velvet and helped Catherine into it.

"How can you be so slow?" Catherine complained as she did it up. "And now my boots! My gloves! My hat! I must take my jewels with me! For Heaven's sake, could anyone be more incompetent?"

Abusing Theola, and fidgeting so that it was difficult to fasten the habit, she was finally dressed and turned to the mirror to adjust her high-crowned hat which was encircled by a gauze veil.

"I cannot think what the troops are doing allowing these revolutionaries to get out of hand," she said.

"Was His Majesty expecting an insurrection of any sort?" Theola asked.

"He told me there might be some trouble," Catherine answered, "but I had no idea my life might be in danger!"

She gave a little scream of fear.

"Oh, Theola, I wish I had not come! I wish I were back in England! I am frightened, do you hear me? Frightened!"

"I am sure it will be all right," Theola answered soothingly. "The King will look after you! After all, he is taking you to safety. Surely his own special guards will protect him?"

"Yes, they all are Austrian," Catherine replied in a tone of relief. "The King told me how he had picked them especially and that he could always rely on them."

"Then you will be all right," Theola assured her, "and you will soon be back here."

"Where can we be going?" Catherine cried. "Supposing I am wounded?"

She was very pale and trembling with fear.

"I am sure His Majesty will look after you," Theola said again.

Catherine was about to reply when there was a shout from the Sitting-Room.

"Catherine! Are you ready?"

It was the Duke who called, and Catherine, picking up her riding-gloves, answered:

"I am coming, Papa."

She ran across the bed-room and into the Sitting-Room without speaking another word to Theola.

"Come on! The King is waiting. I cannot imagine why women take so long to change their clothes!" Theola heard the Duke say sharply.

"You are coming with us, Papa?" Catherine asked.

"Yes, of course," the Duke replied. "Now hurry! The horses are waiting at a side-door."

They must have left the room as he was speaking because his voice died away and Theola stood still amongst the mess that Catherine had left behind her.

Her gown, petticoats, slippers, her long white gloves, and the wreath from her hair all lay on the floor.

Over the chair hung the pink riding-habit which Theola had lifted from the wardrobe first. The drawers of the dressing-table were open and Catherine's special toilet requisites had been scattered about while she searched for her jewellery and stuffed it into the pockets of her habit.

Automatically Theola started to pick up everything and put them in their proper places.

She wondered where the King and Catherine were being taken and guessed it would be Greece.

Zanthos, she knew, was only about two hours' ride from the border, while it would be much further and over far-more-difficult country if they tried to reach Albania.

Looking at the map before she had come to Kavōnia, she had realised that while the country was more or less encircled by mountains, those on the Albanian side were far higher and less accessible.

This was doubtless why the Turks had never attempted to add Kavōnia to the Ottoman Empire.

The only alternative would be to take a ship from the Port of Khévea. But Theola guessed that the revolutionaries would doubtless have thought of that and would be waiting to intercept the King if he attempted to escape on the main road to the Port.

Someone with intelligence, Theola thought, must have decided that the only chance the King had of getting away would be for him to ride across country.

She wondered how many people were in the party which included Catherine and the Duke.

She did not at all resent being left behind.

It was, she thought, what she might have expected, and after all, as the Duke had said, she was English and therefore it was unlikely that the revolutionaries would shoot her, if she had time to proclaim her nationality.

"I should really drape myself in the Union Jack!" she told herself with a smile.

Then she thought that perhaps her situation was not very amusing, but rather frightening.

At the same time, she was quite certain that however indifferent the Duke might be about her welfare, he would in fact have instructed someone in the Palace to look after her.

There were numerous officials of every sort and there were also Courtiers and their wives, none of whom would wish to offend their future Queen by neglecting her cousin and Lady-in-Waiting.

'It is no use my going to look for anyone,' Theola thought sensibly. 'They know I am here and perhaps when the situation outside is clearer someone will tell me what to do.'

Having finally tidied Catherine's bed-room, she walked into the Sitting-Room and for the first time thought she might explore the Royal Suite.

The rooms were intercommunicating so that the King and Queen had no need to go into the main corridor, where there were always sentries on guard.

Quietly, in case anyone was on duty and would question her behaviour, Theola opened the door through which the Duke had entered Catherine's Sitting-Room.

It led, she found, into a very attractive Ante-Chamber, small but decorated with a delightful collection of Meissen china.

Theola decided that when she had time she would

inspect it thoroughly, but now she was on a journey of exploration and opened the door on the other side of the Ante-Chamber.

This, she found, led into the King's Sitting-Room.

It was far larger than the Queen's and much more sombre, with a huge gilt-handled desk on which reposed a most impressive gold ink-pot.

On two walls of the room hung very fine tapestries and on the others the inevitable pictures of the Hapsburgs, all of them, Theola thought, having the same aloof, disdainful air which was characteristic of King Ferdinand.

On one side of the mantelpiece there was a portrait of the Empress Elizabeth.

She had been described as the most beautiful woman in Europe, which Theola was sure was true.

But there were rumours that she was very unhappy in the stiff and restrictive Court at Vienna.

'I am not surprised,' Theola thought, looking at the Empress's lovely face and thinking that perhaps Franz-Joseph was as pompous as King Ferdinand.

She walked across the room to the desk and wondered if the King had ever signed an Act of Mercy for his subjects.

Since coming to Kavōnia she had found it hard not to feel that the Court was entirely isolated from the people outside.

She kept remembering the terrible poverty of the house into which she had taken the injured child, the narrow, squalid streets with their closed shutters, and the silence which was in such vivid contrast to the rest of the city.

She wished she had had a chance to speak with Captain Petlos of what had happened, but she had had no opportunity of being alone with him since she had arrived in Zanthos.

There was no doubt that he had known who Alexius Vasilas was from the very moment he had come to collect the child.

55

Theola remembered him saying in a whisper that she had not been intended to hear:

"Are you crazy? If you are recognised you will be shot!"

Captain Petlos would have been given his orders like the rest of the Army to shoot the revolutionary on sight, and yet he had not only disobeyed but even pretended to be the father of the child.

'Perhaps Alexius Vasilas really is the child's father?' Theola wondered. Then she thought it unlikely.

The little girl had been quite ordinary in appearance, with the attractiveness of youth but not with outstandingly beautiful features as she might have been expected to inherit from such a father.

But if he was no relation, why had Alexius Vasilas concerned himself so deeply with a child who had been knocked down by chance in the street?

There was no explanation for this, Theola thought, unless he believed himself responsible for the people who supported him.

It was all very puzzling, and yet he must at this moment have at his command a large enough force of Kavōnians to frighten the King away from his Palace when it might have been expected that His Majesty would stand his ground and rally the Army round him.

The clock on the mantelpiece chimed the hour and Theola realised that it was growing late. It was in fact after eleven o'clock.

No-one had come to find her and she wondered if, after all, her Uncle had forgotten to mention that she had been left behind and the Courtiers and other officials in the Palace had either retired to bed or left the building.

It was an explanation that Theola had not thought of before.

Could everybody have gone? It seemed unlikely, but now that she thought of it, everything seemed unnaturally quiet.

She walked to the window and pulled aside the heavy velvet curtains to look out.

The King's Sitting-Room overlooked the garden, not the front of the Palace, and it was impossible to see anything but the shadowy outlines of the statues which embellished the terraces and the sky strewn with stars.

She stood looking up and thought how small and insignificant the starry Heavens made the world seem beneath.

Perhaps Heaven existed in one of the other worlds far away from this one, and between them there could be no real communication.

And yet she felt certain that her father and mother were not far from her.

How could her father not know that she was near Greece, the land he had loved beyond all others?

"Whatever happens, Papa," Theola said, "I must not be afraid. I must not be a coward or scream—even if I am hurt."

She was well aware that Catherine had not behaved with any courage, although the soldiers who escorted her and the King to wherever they were going would expect their Royalty to be brave whatever dangers encompassed them.

"Perhaps I should go and see if there is anyone about," Theola said to herself, and walked back into the centre of the room.

She had reached the King's desk when suddenly there were the sounds of voices and heavy footsteps in the corridor outside.

She stood still, listening. Then, so unexpectedly that she started, the double doors at the far end of the room were flung open violently and several soldiers with their muskets raised stood in the doorway.

Theola felt her heart give a frightened leap, but she forced herself to stand very still, steadying herself against the desk and at the same time raising her head proudly.

The soldiers looked round the room as if they were searching for someone and Theola saw that they wore the uniform of the Kavōnian Army.

She was just about to speak to them in their own language when a man appeared between them.

He was wearing a uniform and Theola looked at him incredulously.

She could hardly believe it, but it was Alexius Vasilas!

She forgot what she had been about to say and could only stare at him as he advanced towards her.

"Where is the King?" he asked in German.

Even as he spoke she knew that he recognised her.

"Where is the King?" he asked again, but now in English:

"He has left the Palace," Theola replied.

"How long ago?"

"Why are you here? And why are you dressed like that?" Theola enquired.

"I represent the Kavōnian people," he answered, "and I am now in command of the Kavōnian Army."

He spoke impatiently, as if he had no wish to answer questions. Then before Theola could speak he said:

"I must ask you to tell me at what hour the King left the Palace."

"A long time ago."

"An hour—two hours?"

Alexius Vasilas snapped the question at Theola and after a moment's thought and a glance at the clock she replied:

"Perhaps an hour and a half. I am not certain. I did not see him actually leave."

"I gather his future wife went with him?"

"That is correct," Theola agreed.

"They left you behind! Why?"

"I am of no special consequence," Theola answered, "and besides, my Uncle was quite certain that being British I would be safe."

"But of course!" Alexius Vasilas replied with a twist of his lips and a sarcastic note in his voice. "Your countrymen are not likely to concern themselves with our problems even if they hear of them. At the same time, a British citizen is of course inviolate!"

"I am grateful for your assurance on that point," Theola said.

"You will be safe but you will confine yourself to your room, which I imagine is not this one."

"My bed-room is next to the Queen's," Theola replied.

"Then you will remain in the Queen's Suite," Alexius Vasilas said. "I will make arrangements where you are concerned later. Until then, stay in the rooms allotted to you."

He spoke, Theola thought, as if he were ordering about a raw recruit.

Because she felt that once again he was looking at her with contempt and dislike, she dropped him a small curtsey and, holding her head very high, walked slowly from the King's room and into the Ante-Chamber.

As she went she could hear Alexius Vasilas giving sharp orders, and although she could not understand them she supposed that he intended to try to intercept the King and Catherine and was sending soldiers to do so.

She entered the Queen's Sitting-Room, closed the communicating door, and sat down in a chair.

It was quite obvious that Alexius Vasilas had achieved a *coup d'état* and that, as he had said, a large part of the Army was now under his command.

This meant that the King, in all probability, could rely only on his Austrian-born troops.

There were, however, a number of mercenaries in the Army, as Captain Petlos had said, and they were more likely to be loyal to the reigning Monarch than to join an insurrection.

There was of course always the chance that King

George of Greece might wish to support a brother-Monarch.

'There will be a lot of blood-shed!' Theola thought, imagining how horrifying it would be if instead of the wedding-festivities, gay with flowers, flags, and bunting, civil war should rage in Zanthos.

It was impossible to believe that every Kavōnian would support Alexius Vasilas.

There were many, especially shop-keepers, craftsmen, and those who pandered to the luxury of the Palace, who would have a great deal to lose if there were no longer a King living extravagantly.

"How I hate wars . . . all wars!" Theola told herself.

She wondered why Alexius Vasilas, who looked like Apollo, could not try to rule as the god had done, without an Army, without a Navy, but by the power of his beauty which evoked love.

She sat in the Sitting-Room, realising that it was growing later and later, but she was afraid to go to bed in case Alexius Vasilas should wish to speak to her again.

It would be extremely embarrassing if he demanded to see her when she was in fact in bed.

At the same time, she felt very tired.

She had had a long day attending to Catherine, and the shock of what had happened and the nagging fear of the future, even though she tried to laugh it away, made her feel exhausted.

She was dozing in the chair when there came a knock at the dorr.

She sat up hastily as the door opened, but it was not Alexius Vasilas who stood there but the elderly maid who had attended her since she had come to the Palace.

Her name was Magara, and after so many hours of being alone Theola was delighted to see her.

"Magara!" she exclaimed. "I am so glad you have come to me! What is happening? What is going on outside the Palace?"

Magara shut the door but before she did so Theola had a glimpse of a sentry outside the door.

"The General sent me to you, *Fraulein*," she replied.

"The General?" Theola questioned.

"General Vasilas, *Fraulein*."

"He is a General?" Theola asked.

"He is in command of the Army and they have taken over the city, *Fraulein*."

Magara smiled.

"It is good news, *Fraulein*. We are all very happy! It is what we always prayed would happen!"

"You wanted a revolution?" Theola asked incredulously.

"We wanted Alexius Vasilas in his proper place. This is where he belongs, *Fraulein*."

Then Magara looked frightened, as if she felt that she had said too much.

"I should not be speaking like this," she said in a low voice. "You must forgive me, *Fraulein*, if I forget myself."

"I want you to tell me the truth."

"The General said I was to stay here and look after you."

"He does not wish to see me himself?"

"No, *Fraulein*. The General is very busy. He is not at this moment in the Palace."

There was a knock at the door and Magara went to answer it.

"I ordered you a warm drink before I came upstairs, *Fraulein*."

"That was very kind of you," Theola said.

Magara took the drink from someone at the door and now Theola could see that there were two sentries on duty.

'I am a prisoner!' she thought to herself.

At the same time, she thought it was considerate of General Vasilas, if that was what he called himself, to send Magara to attend to her.

She drank the warm drink. It was soothing and now that Magara was with her she was no longer so apprehensive.

"Go to bed, *Fraulein*," Magara suggested. "There will be a great deal of excitement tomorrow, and perhaps there will be fighting!"

"I hope not!" Theola exclaimed.

"I hope not as well," Magara agreed. "When I was a child my father was killed in a revolution, and because our house was burnt over our heads my little brother died of the cold when we escaped into the mountains."

"Do you think the King has a large enough force to fight General Vasilas?" Theola asked.

"I do not know, *Fraulein*," Magara answered. "Why did you not go with your English relatives?"

Theola smiled.

"Quite simply because they did not want me, Magara. The King was in a hurry and he could take only Lady Catherine and the Duke with him."

She felt that it sounded like a criticism and added:

"There must be plenty of people left in the Palace who can look after me. Where is everybody?"

"Many have gone already, *Fraulein*, and many more are packing. The General has ordered them out of the Palace."

"All of them?" Theola questioned.

"Everyone who is Austrian, *Fraulein*, and that is everyone except the servants."

Theola drew in her breath.

Alexius Vasilas was certainly being ruthless.

"They are going without protest?" she asked after a moment, thinking of all the elaborate and ornate uniforms which had been worn by the Court officials.

"They have already surrendered their swords and any arms they carried, *Fraulein*. There is a huge pile in the centre of the Hall and a number of sentries to guard it."

Theola did not reply and after a moment Magara said in the tone of an English Nanny:

"Come along and get into bed, *Fraulein*. You will sleep in the Queen's bed, and, if you will permit me, I will occupy your room."

Theola was about to protest that the Queen's bed was far too grand for her. Then she was sure that Magara would never presume on her position and could sleep only if she was permitted to use the Lady-in-Waiting's room.

"Yes, of course, Magara," she said aloud. "That will be sensible."

She thought that it would be impossible to sleep, but the warm drink made her drift away into unconsciousness almost as soon as her head touched the pillow.

* * *

Theola awoke with a start to hear the sound of marching feet beneath her window and sharp commands being shouted. After a moment she realised that the sentries were being changed and it must be seven o'clock in the morning.

She intended going to the window, but as she sat up in bed Magara came into the room carrying a tray.

"I thought the soldiers would awaken you, *Fraulein*," she said, "so I have brought you some breakfast."

Theola glanced at the fresh crisp rolls on her tray, the pat of golden butter, and the comb of honey. She could smell the fragrant coffee, and realised that she had been brought exactly the same breakfast she had received every day since she had been at the Palace.

As if Magara sensed her unspoken question, she said:

"The kitchen-staff are working normally. All the cooks, with the exception of the Chief Chef, are Kavōnian."

"And the Chief Chef?" Theola enquired.

"He has disappeared, *Fraulein*. We think he must have gone with the King. He was a very timid man!"

Theola laughed.

63

"What is happening, Magara?" she asked as she poured out her coffee.

"Many, many things, *Fraulein*. There are soldiers everywhere with new officers giving orders."

"I imagine they are Kavōnian," Theola said.

"Followers of the General, *Fraulein*, who have been with him all the time he has been hiding in the mountains."

"Is that where he has been?" Theola asked.

"Sometimes he has come to the city, *Fraulein*. But it was always dangerous—very dangerous—and we were afraid when we saw him."

"You knew he was here?"

"He brought us hope, *Fraulein*. Hope that one day we would be free!"

Theola buttered her roll before she asked:

"Is General Vasilas married?"

"No, *Fraulein*. We have always thought he will marry his cousin, the Princess Athene Vasilas, but how can a man marry when he has no home and there is a price on his head?"

"Have the Austrians offered money to anyone who would betray him?" Theola questioned.

"A very big sum! Any man who earned it would have been rich for life," Magara replied. "But no-one would betray Alexius Vasilas. He has always been our true leader, our only hope for the future."

"And now?" Theola asked.

"We are all very happy, *Fraulein*, but afraid—yes, afraid that we have not enough arms, enough guns with which to defend ourselves."

Theola did not speak and after a moment Magara said passionately:

"You will understand, *Fraulein*, we are very poor! We have no money! Pistols, bullets, muskets, and gunpowder are expensive—very expensive! And yet, every year we have all of us given what we can afford."

"You mean you have collected for this for a long time?" Theola asked.

"For nine years, *Fraulein*. Ever since Alexius Vasilas came back to Kavōnia."

"He went away?"

"He and his mother were exiled after the King came to the throne. It was not because of anything he had done, *Fraulein*. He was only a boy, but the King was afraid that the people would follow a Vasilas."

"So they were sent away," Theola said.

"The Princess died, I think it was in Italy, *Fraulein*. When he was a man Alexius Vasilas returned."

"And that was nine years ago?"

"Yes, *Fraulein*. He was twenty-one and when we learnt he was here the hearts of all Kavōnians were raised. It was like a light shining in the darkness!"

That was what she might have expected, Theola thought. It was light that Alexius Vasilas would bring to the people who trusted him.

It was impossible to stay in bed with so many exciting things happening and she longed to be part of them. But when she was dressed Magara told her she was not allowed to leave the Sitting-Room.

"May I not at least go to see what is happening in the Court-Yard on the other side of the Palace?" Theola begged.

Magara asked the sentries but they refused.

"They have their orders, *Fraulein*. You may not leave the room."

"I understand," Theola said.

But she was disappointed, and the quiet sunlit gardens that she could see from her windows were a very poor compensation for the excitement that must be taking place on the other side of the great building.

There was nothing for her to do, and while she tried to read some of the books in the Sitting-Room, which were all in German, it was impossible to concentrate her mind on anything but the revolution.

A dozen time she sent Magara downstairs to see what she could discover.

The maid would come back with scraps of information which Theola had to interpret like the pieces of a jig-saw puzzle, which together made a general picture of the whole.

"All the Austrians are gone, *Fraulein*, every one of them!" Magara cried on one occasion. "The ladies are crying and wailing, and the gentlemen are cursing!"

"Where have they gone to?"

"The General has arranged for a ship to carry them to Naples. What annoyed them was that they were allowed to take so few of their possessions with them. Many have grown very rich since they have been in Kavōnia."

"How have they done that?" Theola asked.

"There were few who would not accept bribes, *Fraulein*."

"But who bribed them, and for what purposes?" Theola asked.

"The shop-keepers, the manufacturers, the men who came from other countries bringing goods that might interest the King. No-one could get into the Royal presence unless they were helped by the Gentlemen-in-Waiting, His Majesty's secretaries, and oh, many, many people!"

"Well, I only hope that what they have left behind will be put to good use," Theola said.

"It will, *Fraulein*, you can be sure of that. The General has threatened that anyone who loots a house or any other place will be severely punished."

"And they will obey him?" Theola asked, thinking of the stories she had read of soldiers looting, burning, and devastating the countries they conquered.

"They will obey him," Magara said simply, "because he understands their feelings and how we have all suffered these past years."

Gradually Theola came to understand that when Magara spoke of suffering it was in fact no exaggeration.

Any man who owned a small holding or a farm, she learnt, had been required to give half his crop and half his live-stock every year to the Bailiff who represented the King.

Young men were conscripted into the Kavōnian Army at the age of seventeen, and when a man's parents were too old to till the soil they owned, the land was confiscated.

Food was expensive, and those who lived in the city were often near starvation simply because they could not earn enough to pay the exorbitant prices charged in the market-place because the traders had to pay so much rent for their stalls or stands.

The whole country, Theola realised, had been run entirely for the King's benefit: whenever he wanted anything, like building the Palace or another Hunting-Lodge in the mountains, which she gathered was practically finished, the money was raised almost entirely from the peasants.

No wonder they looked on Alexius Vasilas as a deliverer who would strike away their chains of bondage and make them free, as they had been before an Austrian King came to the throne.

Magara told her of the great rejoicing there was now in Zanthos.

"The people dance and sing all day," she said. "Even the soldiers wear flowers behind their ears and in their caps, and the General has arranged for food to be given to those who are too poor to buy any."

It was very frustrating, Theola thought, not to be able to see what was happening or take any part in it.

She ate the dinner that Magara served her, and although it was well cooked she was not hungry and pushed her plate away after a few mouthfuls.

"You are not hungry, *Fraulein?*" Magara asked reproachfully.

"I want to see the General," Theola said. "I cannot be shut up here indefinitely."

"He is very busy, *Fraulein.* Perhaps tomorrow he will have time to talk to you."

Theola could not help feeling that tomorrow might be another day when she would sit alone in this comfortable and impressive prison, but still a prisoner.

She was not mistaken. The next day passed exactly like the first.

"What is happening? Do tell me what is happening, Magara," she begged.

"I understand, *Fraulein*," Magara said after she had served luncheon, "that the King reached the border and the troops who support him are concentrated there."

"Where?" Theola asked.

"Where Kavōnia joins Greece, *Fraulein*. That is what one of the soldiers told us, but of course he knew very little, and the General does not confide in everyone."

"I wish he would confide in me," Theola said. "Do try to find out more, Magara."

Magara did her best but was not very successful.

"Is there fighting?" Theola asked.

"I think there has been a little fighting amongst some of the mercenaries who wanted to join the King and the Kavōnians who opposed them, but it was not very serious."

Later in the afternoon Magara told Theola:

"I understand, *Fraulein*, the General has given orders for everyone outside Zanthos to come inside the city. He says they will be safer there and the farmers are driving in their flocks. They are congregated in the market-place."

"I wonder why he is doing that," Theola said.

Magara could not enlighten her, for although she was an intelligent woman she could only report what she had heard or what she had seen, and Theola had to puzzle out the reasons for herself.

It was growing late in the afternoon and Theola had eaten her dinner when through the open window she heard the sound of crying.

It was a warm night and she leaned out, wondering where the noise could be coming from.

"I can hear children," she said to Magara, who was putting away the table-cloth.

"Yes, *Fraulein,* there are children in the room below this."

"Children?" Theola questioned.

"There were several who were lost or wounded during the fighting."

"I did not know there had been any."

"There was a little, *Fraulein.* When the General entered the city the Austrian guards fired at him, but when they saw how many of the soldiers were no longer serving the King they surrendered or ran away."

"And children were hurt during the process?" Theola asked as if to herself.

"The General had them brought here until their parents can be found. There are not many of them," Magara said.

She picked up the tray.

"If you have no further use for me, *Fraulein,* I would like to go out for a little while. There is dancing and many celebrations to watch."

"But of course, Magara," Theola replied. "Enjoy yourself! I wish I could come with you."

"The General would not approve of that, *Fraulein!*" Magara replied.

She curtseyed and, going to the door, knocked so that the sentries could open it for her.

Theola gave a little sigh.

If the General had wished to punish her for being who she was, he was certainly succeeding.

She was finding it almost intolerable to be alone and to have little idea of what was happening outside these two elaborate and baroque rooms.

'Papa would be ashamed of me for not being self-sufficient and finding a message in the silence,' she thought.

She walked to the window and drew back the curtains.

As she did so there was a flash in the sky and she

realised from the noise that fireworks were being set off in the town.

Occasionally there was another flash, and she knew that they could be seen only from the other side of the Palace.

She looked up at the starlit sky, then at the garden, and smelt the fragrance of the night-scented flowers. Once again she heard the children crying below.

Now it seemed more insistent than it had been earlier; in fact one child was screaming!

'Surely someone is attending to them,' Theola thought.

She listened, but there was no respite as there would have been if the child had been picked up and comforted.

She could not believe that the General would have left them there without an attendant, but whoever was looking after them was not very effective.

'I wonder if I could get to them?' she thought to herself.

She remembered that in the bed-room she had first used, the door opened onto a side-passage and not straight onto the corridor as did those of the King's and Queen's Suites.

She thought it possible that while General Vasilas had remembered to post sentries outside her door, he might have overlooked the door of the Lady-in-Waiting's room.

She went through her bed-room and into Magara's.

The door into the passage was unlocked and she opened it very slowly and quietly.

There were no sentries outside and she let herself out, closing the door behind her.

The passage led into the main corridor, but there was another passage opposite, and this, Theola could see, was unguarded.

On tip-toe she went to the corner of the wall and peeped round it.

The sentries outside her Sitting-Room were deep in conversation. They were quite some way away and the corridor was dark.

Theola took off her slippers, and holding them in her hand she drew a deep breath and ran.

She reached the other side of the corridor and waited apprehensively.

There was no sound except for the continued murmur of the sentries and she realised that they had not seen her.

Now she had to find her way down to the next floor. It was not difficult.

Moving away from the centre of the building where there was the Grand Staircase, she walked down several smaller passages and finally found some secondary stairs.

These were hung with pictures of Austrian Monarchs, which suggested that they were used by the Palace officials.

Quickly she ran downstairs to find more passages which were unguarded.

Because she had a good sense of direction it was not difficult to find a way to the rooms which she knew lay directly beneath the Queen's Suite.

She half-expected there would be sentries on the ground floor also, and she was moving slowly in the shadows when she saw one. But he had his back to her and was facing the Hall, where Theola was certain there would be other sentries.

She suspected that they would not be taking their duties very seriously. For after all, she told herself, there were only the children and herself to guard.

Now she could hear the children crying and a moment later she was in the room with them.

What must have been a large office had been converted into a dormitory.

There were three ordinary-sized single beds, three mattresses on the floor, and a cot which had been painted elaborately with the Royal Arms.

There was no sign of any grown-up in the room and the children were all crying. She went from one to another until she found the reason.

The child who was screaming had had his head roughly bandaged and the bandage had slipped over his eyes.

As soon as Theola adjusted it, the child stopped crying and clung to her, saying over and over again in the Kavōnian tongue:

"Mother! I want my mother!"

"She will be coming soon," Theola said soothingly. "Try to go to sleep. She would want you to rest."

In the next bed, a little girl who had hurt her hands had got the bandages entangled with the bed-clothes and was struggling to free herself.

The baby in the cot was obviously hungry.

Someone had put a bottle in his mouth, but it had slipped to one side and the baby was far too young to be able to lift it back to his lips.

The milk in the bottle seemed cold as Theola put the teat back in the child's mouth, and she would have liked to warm it. But he sucked at it greedily, obviously too hungry to be particular.

Theola propped up the bottle carefully so that it would not slip again, and then went to another of the beds.

The other children were crying because they were upset by the noise the others were making and were frightened.

She soothed them, tucked them up, talking to them all the time, telling them that their mothers would be coming soon and they must be good until they could go home.

In a very short space of time there was silence in the room and most of the children were asleep.

Theola was just making sure that the bandage on the head of the first child she had tended could not slip again when she heard a sound in the doorway.

She turned to see a sentry. He stood watching her.

"The children were crying," she said in Kavōnian, "so I came down to look after them."

The man did not answer but continued to stare at her.

"They are all right now," Theola said, "but surely there should be someone with them?"

"She's gone dancing," the soldier said.

He slurred his words and Theola realised that he had been drinking. His cap had slipped to the back of his head and he was carrying his musket at an angle. He had undone the top buttons of his tunic.

"Well . . . I think the children will be quiet . . . until she comes back," Theola said.

She looked doubtfully at the soldier again, feeling that he was really not the sort of person who should be in charge of them.

He was a stocky man of about thirty, with dark skin and hair that was far too long for a regular soldier.

'He is doubtless,' Theola thought, 'a follower of General Vasilas who has never worn a uniform until this moment.'

She took a last look round at the children.

They were all very quiet and the baby had fallen asleep, still sucking at his bottle.

She walked towards the door, saying:

"Perhaps I had better go back to my own room."

The soldier did not move.

He swayed a little as he stood and the look in his eyes made Theola feel suddenly uneasy.

"Please let me pass," she said.

He made no effort to obey her, and feeling that he must be too drunk to understand what she was saying, she tried to squeeze her way past him.

As she did so he dropped his musket and reached out to put his arms round her.

"Let me go! How dare you touch me?" she cried, and found to her horror that he was very strong.

He held her closely against him and now she could

73

smell the wine on his breath as she fought to free herself.

But nothing she could do was in any way effective against the manner in which he was holding her.

She struggled and twisted, but he dragged her across the room to where there was an empty mattress.

"No! No!" Theola cried. "Let me go!"

He did not answer, but half-dragging, half carrying, her, he tumbled her backwards onto the mattress and she screamed as she fell.

He flung himself on top of her, and thinking he was about to kiss her, she turned her face away.

But instead he dragged at her gown, tearing it with brutal hands as she screamed and screamed again.

Her breasts were now bare, and as she felt him tearing at her skirt she thought despairingly that she must die at the horror of what he was about to do.

Suddenly there was an explosion which seemed to reverberate deafeningly in Theola's ears.

She felt the man slump forward against her and for a moment lost consciousness from the hard impact of his body.

Then someone was dragging the soldier off her and instinctively she put up her hands to her bare breasts.

It was impossible to think, almost impossible to realise that she had been saved.

She heard a thump as the body of the man who had lain on top of her was thrown to the floor. Then a voice harshly said in English:

"What are you doing here? And why are you not in your own room?"

She was still lying on the mattress and she looked up into the face of Alexius Vasilas!

She was too frightened and shocked to answer him, and after a moment he took hold of her arms and pulled her to her feet.

Her legs would not support her and she swayed against him, her face hidden against his shoulder.

"I gave orders you were to stay in the Queen's

Suite," he said sharply. "Why have you disobeyed me?"

He waited for an answer and in a voice she hardly recognised as her own, Theola managed to say:

"The . . . children . . . were . . . crying."

She felt without raising her head that the General looked round and saw that there was no attendant in the room.

"I gave orders for someone to look after them," he said, and she heard the anger in his voice.

"I think the . . . woman has gone . . . dancing," she murmured.

"I will deal with this," he said. "Can you walk?"

"I . . . I think . . . so," Theola answered.

She tried to move, then felt as if the room was going black and the floor was rising up to meet her.

She felt his arms go round her as she fell. . . .

* * *

It seemed a long time later when she realised that she was being carried upstairs.

There was a feeling of protection and security in the General's arms which swept away her fears, and the darkness was gradually receding from her mind.

'He has . . . saved me!' she thought to herself. 'He . . . has saved me!'

Without opening her eyes, she knew they must have reached the corridor of the floor above. She heard the sentries come to attention, then one of them must have opened the door and the General carried her into the Queen's bed-room.

Theola opened her eyes as he set her down on the bed against the pillows, keeping her hands protectively over her naked breasts, ashamed that he should see her in such a state.

"Are you all right?" he asked gravely.

"Quite . . . all right . . . now."

"Then change your gown," he said. "I will come back to you when I have seen to the children."

He turned and went from the room and she could

hear him speaking sharply to the sentries in the corridor outside.

She lay for a moment trying to get her breath, realising with horror what had happened and how the General had only just saved her in time.

Then she remembered that he was returning, and hastily she rose to go to the wardrobe to find another gown.

Magara had moved her gowns in with Catherine's, and when she opened the inlaid doors of the wardrobe, Catherine's frocks fluttered in the breeze, soft and lovely as the spring flowers.

Theola looked at her own heavy, ugly dresses and decided that she felt too exhausted to put one on.

Instead, she took from a hanger a white wrap which Catherine wore when she had her hair brushed.

It was plain, with large sleeves, like a monk's robe. There were no buttons or hooks to fasten. It crossed over the breast and tied with a sash at the side.

Theola threw her torn gown into a corner, feeling that she could not bear to look at it and remember the soldier's hands tearing it from her neck.

She had heard and read that this was the way soldiers behaved in war, but she had never expected it to happen to her. Now she knew how terrifying it was for a woman to encounter violence and be alone without the protection of a man.

She tidied her hair automatically and went into the Sitting-Room to wait for the General.

She felt her heart beating unaccountably at the thought of talking to him.

It had already been embarrassing enough to know that he despised her and to remember the contempt in his eyes.

But that was before she had deliberately disobeyed his orders and left the safety of her room to involve herself with the soldier whom he had shot.

To have been instrumental in causing the death of a man was to Theola so horrible that she could hardly contemplate it.

But the General had killed to save her from being ravished and she knew that she must thank him, however difficult it was to do so.

It seemed to her that she waited a long time before she heard the sentries come to attention and there was a knock on the door.

"Come . . . in!" she said.

She felt as if the words were strangled in her throat.

He entered the room, closing the door behind him, and she thought that while he looked stern and uncompromising he was in fact devastatingly good-looking.

'I know Papa would have said he looked like Apollo,' she thought to herself.

Then she rose nervously to her feet to curtsey as he reached her side.

"You are feeling better, Miss Waring?"

His voice was not angry, she thought in relief.

"I . . . I am quite all right and I must . . . thank you . . ." she began.

"There is no reason to thank me," Alexius Vasilas said. "I am only deeply apologetic that you should have been insulted by a Kavōnian."

He paused to add:

"At the same time, you will appreciate that if you disobey my orders, that is the sort of situation in which you may find yourself."

"I . . . I am . . . sorry," Theola said.

"We are at war, Miss Waring," the General went on, "and when men are at war they become excitable and their emotions are inflamed one way or another. That is why women should never be involved, but remain in safety."

"But . . . the children were . . . crying," Theola said, as if she must explain her action.

"That is also regrettable," the General said. "The woman I put in charge of them will be severely reprimanded. To set your mind at rest, I have found another, more-reliable person who will stay with them through the night. I hope that by the morning their parents will have claimed them."

"I am ... glad about that," Theola said.

"I think you should sit down," the General suggested. "You have been through an unfortunate experience. The sooner you get to bed, the better!"

"I wanted to ... talk to ... you," Theola said.

"And I have certain things to say to you," the General answered.

As she seated herself he sat down on a chair opposite her.

She thought that despite the unusual circumstances in which they found themselves he seemed very much at his ease.

"You will be relieved to know, Miss Waring," he began after a moment, "that your cousin, Lady Catherine, and the King have both reached Greece safely."

"I thought that was where they would go."

"I believed you when you told me that you did not know."

"But that was only what I guessed. They were not likely to confide in me!"

"I cannot understand why you did not accompany them. After all, your Uncle was included in the King's party, and I should not have thought it difficult for them to include one extra person."

"I ... I think my Uncle's only thought was for his daughter to reach safety," Theola answered.

"But you are his niece!"

"He is not particularly ... proud of me," Theola said without thinking.

She realised she had been indiscreet as the General raised his eye-brows.

She felt that he was waiting for an explanation and after a moment she said:

"I am the poor relation. I expect even in Kavōnia you know what that means. And such are easily ... dispensable!"

She spoke without bitterness, almost with a note of

āmusement in her voice, and after a moment the General said:

"I can hardly understand that. I assure you there are few Kavōnians who would abandon their relatives in such circumstances."

There was nothing Theola could say to that and after a moment's silence the General said:

"I have here something which belongs to you."

Theola looked at him in surprise and he drew an object from the pocket of his tunic and held it out to her.

As she bent forward to take it from him she realised it was the gold coin she had left for the injured child.

"I had intended to return it when we met and say that we in Kavōnia are in no need of your charity," the General said. "But now I think you could ill afford such a generous gift."

Theola looked down at the gold coin as it lay in her hand.

"It belonged to my father," she said. "It represents a third of everything I possess in the world."

"And yet you gave it to that child. And why did you tend her when she was knocked down by your carriage?"

Theola hesitated a moment, then said:

"Because my father loved Greece, and because it was the most wonderful experience of my life to come to Kavōnia."

There was an unmistakable little throb in her voice as she went on:

"I have been appalled at the contrasts I have seen here: the extravagance in this Palace and the poverty outside it. I have heard how badly your people have been treated and I would like to help them."

"As you were trying to help the children tonight, when they were crying and frightened," the General said.

"How is the little girl who was injured by our carriage?"

"A doctor tended her and her leg is healing."

"Oh, I am glad. I understand there is no hospital."

"Not now," the General replied. "But there used to be. It was pulled down when the King wished to extend the gardens of the Palace."

Theola gave a little sigh.

"You will build another?"

"If I am in the position to do so."

She looked at him apprehensively.

"You think there is a chance that the King may be ... reinstated?"

"I understand that those who support him do not intend to give up without a fight," the General replied. "They may not be able to defeat us, but we must be prepared."

"Yes, of course," Theola said. "And may I help?"

"I will have to think about it, Miss Waring," the General said. "You are aware that you must be protected."

He rose to his feet as he spoke.

"In times of war," he said, "a beautiful woman is always a liability!"

Taken completely by surprise at the compliment, Theola stared at him wide-eyed. Then before she could reply, before she could rise, he turned and walked across the room and the door closed behind him.

She stood staring after him, the gold coin she had given the child clutched in her hand.

"A beautiful woman is always a liability!" she repeated to herself.

She found it incredible that he should think her beautiful!

CHAPTER FOUR

In the morning, Magara looked grave and Theola asked:

"What is the matter? Is something happening that you have not told me?"

"We are just a little worried, *Fraulein*," Magara answered. "There are rumours that the King's troops intend to attack the city! But you know how people talk."

She made an expressive gesture with her hands and Theola asked quickly:

"The General has said nothing?"

"Nothing, *Fraulein*, and that is what makes me think the people are gossiping because they are afraid."

She paused before she said:

"Many in the city were so certain that the Lady Catherine was the Princess from across the sea who was to bring us peace and prosperity."

"You mean that is what their Prime Minister told them?" Theola asked.

"Yes, that is what we were told," Magara agreed.

Theola dressed and went into the Sitting-Room.

She wondered if the General realised how hard it was to be confined to a house when outside the sun was warm and the flowers were so beautiful.

She longed to walk in the garden, to feel free of the overpowering atmosphere of the Queen's Suite and the faces of the Hapsburgs, who, she was certain, were looking down at her with disapproval.

It must have been nearly noon when she heard a knock at the door, and thinking it was perhaps her luncheon, she called out, "Come in!" without turning her head.

She heard someone enter; then, as Magara did not speak, she looked round and saw with surprise that it was the General.

For a moment she was still and the sunshine coming through the window haloed the very fair hair which framed her large, anxious eyes in her heart-shaped face.

"I wish to talk to you, Miss Waring," he said after a moment.

He spoke in a grave voice and she wondered apprehensively what he had to say.

They both moved towards the big satin-covered sofas and arm-chairs which were grouped round the ornate stove which naturally was not lit at this time of year.

The General waited until Theola had seated herself, arranging the skirts of the brown merino gown she was wearing. She was well aware that the gown was too hot for such a warm day.

He looked amazingly handsome in his uniform, but she noticed that it was not embellished with epaulettes such as were worn by the other officers in the Kavōnian Army.

There was a silence and Theola had a feeling that he was choosing his words with care before he said:

"I have a proposition to make to you, Miss Waring, which you may find very strange. But will you believe me when I say that I make it in good faith?"

"Of course."

Theola's eyes were raised to his face and she did not understand the expression in his as he looked at her.

"The situation," the General began, "is that the King's forces under their Austrian officers intend to attack Zanthos."

"Are there enough of them?" Theola asked.

"The People's Army is larger in numbers," the General replied, "but we are desperately short of weapons. Our rifles are obsolete and we have no heavy guns."

His lips tightened before he went on:

"On the other hand, the King's Army is supplied with the latest equipment."

Theola did not speak but clasped her fingers together.

"Knowing the damage they can inflict," the General continued, "I cannot allow them to fight in the streets of Zanthos, which would result in the deaths of many civilians, especially women and children."

"Then what can you do?" Theola asked.

"I intend to intercept the King's forces before they reach the city," the General said, "which means, if there is to be an element of surprise, the Army must leave this evening."

"Surely it would be madness to face them in the open?" Theola asked.

"I have thought of that, Miss Waring," the General said with a faint smile. "Fortunately, on the only road leading here from Greece there is a great deal of mountainous country."

"You mean you will ambush them?"

"That is what I hope to do. Quite frankly, it is our only chance."

He paused before he said:

"I have been frank with you, Miss Waring, in telling you of my plans, which must of course remain completely secret. You must not speak of them even to your maid."

"I am not likely to betray your confidence, General," Theola said quickly.

"I am trusting you as I have trusted no-one else," the General said, "because what I am about to do directly concerns yourself."

"Concerns me?" Theola exclaimed.

"My difficulty, Miss Waring, is to know what to do with you."

She looked at him wide-eyed, and he looked away from her as he continued:

"What happened last night is deeply regrettable, but it is something which happens continually, as you must be aware, when men are at war."

Theola felt the blood rising in her cheeks as she remembered the horror and terror of the soldier lying on top of her and how the General had saved her by killing the man.

"The man who assaulted you was of Albanian blood," the General continued, "and as you may know, the Albanians, especially those who live in the mountains, are a very fiery, undisciplined race."

"Are there ... many like ... him in your ... Army?" Theola asked in a low voice.

"I am grateful for whatever men will follow me—whatever they are like or however uncivilised they may be," the General answered.

"I can ... understand that."

"So you will appreciate the difficulty I have in finding appropriate guards for you here," the General said. "If we are defeated, I would not wish to frighten you by relating how the mercenaries are likely to behave!"

Theola drew in her breath.

There was no need for him to elaborate on what he was saying. She had read of the pillage, the looting, and the outrages committed by Napoleon's Armies in Portugal and in other countries of Europe which the French had conquered.

The spoils of war were a soldier's reward and the women of their enemies were the natural pillage to which they felt entitled.

Theola felt herself tremble as she said:

"Please . . . keep me somewhere . . . safe."

"That is what I wish to do," the General answered, "but there is only one certain way to ensure that no man of the Kavōnian Army would lay a finger on you."

"And what is that?"

"It is that you should belong to me!"

The General was speaking in English, but Theola stared at him as if she felt he could not have meant what he said.

Then he added quickly, as if fearing that she might misinterpret his words:

"I am suggesting, Miss Waring, that we should go through a form of marriage. As my wife you would be safe, in the same way as I have been able to walk unharmed about the city and know that no man would betray me."

"Your . . . wife?" Theola murmured faintly.

"In name only," the General said. "It will be a Civil Marriage, which under the laws of Kavōnia I can as Ruler dissolve as soon as we achieve peace."

He paused to add:

"You will then be able to return to your own country, Miss Waring, none the worse for the experience of having been the wife of a revolutionary."

He rose from his chair to walk across the room.

"It is a question of time," he said. "If there were more time, I could make other arrangements; but as it is, this is the only solution I can suggest, although it means of course some embarrassment for you."

Theola was still, then she said:

"I . . . I think, General, you have another . . . reason for asking me to appear as your wife."

The General stopped pacing the floor, and standing in the centre of the room he gave her a sharp glance.

"Are you being clairvoyant, Miss Waring, or has someone been talking?"

"Magara told me," Theola replied, "that the people are worried because they believed that the Princess who would come from across the sea was Catherine and that she would bring them peace and prosperity."

"The Prime Minister was extremely astute in reviving that old legend," the General conceded. "All our history, Miss Waring, as you can quite imagine, is steeped in mythology, superstition, and legend."

"I am not a Princess," Theola said, and remembered that Catherine had said the same.

"The Prime Minister twisted the original Greek to suit his own purpose," the General answered. "The actual translation, in a long, laborious prophecy which extends over hundreds of years, says:

'At this time a nymph will come from the foam who will save the light from darkness and the people will rejoice in peace.'"

Theola started when General Vasilas said the word "nymph."

She remembered how her father had always told her that while she would never look like Aphrodite, she did in fact look like a Greek nymph.

It seemed to her at that moment almost as if her father were speaking to her, telling her what she must do, helping her because he more than anyone else would have understood the need of the Kavōnians.

Theola drew in her breath.

"I will . . . do as you wish, General, but on one . . . condition."

"What is that?" he asked.

"That I may accompany you when you leave the city."

She saw the surprise in his expression, and thinking he was about to refuse, she quickly said:

"I could not bear to stay here alone, wondering what was happening, trying to guess whether it was the King's Army or yours which would return."

She tried to speak calmly but there was an emotional note in her voice. After a moment the General said:

"I accept your terms. I will arrange for the Civil Marriage to take place in public. That will please the people and they will believe in the good auspices you bring to our country."

"I hope I may do . . . that."

"I see you understand," the General said, "that men fight more bravely when they have faith rather than greed in their hearts."

"That is what you must . . . give them," Theola said quickly.

"That is what I intend to do, with your help!"

Theola rose to her feet.

"I want to help you," she said. "I feel this country was made for . . . happiness."

He did not answer. He only looked at her, and as their eyes met she felt almost as if they were speaking to each other without words.

Then he said abruptly:

"Let me reiterate, Miss Waring, that you can trust me. Our marriage will be nothing but a formality and I can only thank you most sincerely for understanding why it is necessary."

He bowed to her as he finished speaking, walked towards the door, and left the room without looking back.

Only when she was alone did Theola put her hands up to her face and feel that she must be trembling.

It all seemed so incredible—part of a dream! Yet she knew that everything the General had said had been based on common sense.

She had seen the crowds holding up pictures of Catherine, and at the time she had thought it strange that it seemed to mean so much to them.

It had been extremely clever of the Prime Minister to ensure that the King's wedding was a popular success by linking his bride with an ancient legend which Theola was sure was believed by every Kavōnian.

Although they were prepared to follow Alexius Vasilas wherever he might lead them, there would always be some, principally women, who would wonder if because Catherine had left them their hope of peace and prosperity had gone with her.

'They must believe in me!' Theola thought. 'They must be sure that I am the nymph who will really help them.'

She thought the legend was typical of the lovely stories that her father had read to her in Greek.

Aphrodite had been born of the foam of the sea, and the nymph of Kavōnia would undoubtedly take the place in their minds not only of the Goddess of Love, but of the Goddesses of Fertility and Prosperity.

'Under General Vasilas they will find all these things,' Theola thought.

But she shivered when she remembered that the King's Armies were equipped with modern rifles and heavy guns.

She was still standing in the Sitting-Room, thinking of what had occurred, when the door of the bed-room opened and Magara came running towards her.

"Is it true, *Fraulein?* Is it true that you are to be married to the General this evening?"

"It is true!" Theola replied.

"I cannot believe it, *Fraulein,* but it is wonderful news! Marvellous! Just what I would want for you!"

"How did you know?" Theola asked.

"The General told me himself, and now I think he goes to the Square to tell the people. It will make them very happy. They love a marriage, and already some of the women were complaining they had been defrauded because the King's wedding will not now take place."

'At least,' Theola thought to herself, 'they will not

have a Catholic marriage taking place in their Cathedral.'

But she did not say this aloud. Instead she said:

"Magara, I have nothing to wear!"

"Nothing to wear, *Fraulein?*" Magara repeated in surprise. "But the wardrobe is full of dresses, and there is a very beautiful wedding-gown."

"But of course . . . Catherine's!" Theola exclaimed.

She had really forgotten that Catherine's clothes were there and it had never occurred to her that she might wear the things her cousin had left behind.

"I suppose they would fit me," she said doubtfully.

She wondered as she spoke what her Aunt would say if she knew that she was putting on Catherine's wedding-gown to wed a revolutionary.

She could remember too her Uncle's words when he had told her he would never give his permission for her to marry and she was not to become interested in a man or allow a man to become interested in her.

'This is different!' she thought. 'The General is not interested in me as a woman, but only that I can substantiate the legend so that he can inspire his Army to fight more valiantly.'

She thought of how he had said the marriage could easily be dissolved once he had won the war. Then she told herself it was no use being concerned with such details at the moment.

All that really mattered was that the people should believe she was the nymph of the prophecy.

"Let us look at the wedding-dress, Magara," she said.

They went into the bed-room and Magara lifted Catherine's wedding-gown out of the wardrobe.

It was very beautiful and very elaborate.

"I can see that it will be too big in the waist, *Fraulein,*" Magara said in a practical tone, "but I can easily alter that."

It was in fact one of the most exquisite gowns that Theola had ever seen, and she knew that from the

Duchess's point of view it had cost an astronomical sum of money.

Of white crêpe, it was draped with tulle over the front of the skirt, then swept back over a small bustle into a cascade of tulle frills which ended in a long train.

There was a large satin bow low down on the back of the gown and the tulle encircled the top of the bodice.

On Catherine's instructions the dressmaker had added bunches of orange-blossom tied with satin ribbons and decorated with diamanté.

It made the gown glitter and appear exceedingly luxurious, but as she looked at it Theola had the idea that it was not particularly fitting, as she aspired not to be a Queen but a nymph.

"I should be very grateful, Magara, if when you take in the waist you will also remove all the flowers and ribbons."

"But, *Fraulein,* they are very pretty!" Magara protested.

"They are too elaborate!" Theola said firmly.

"I will do as you wish, *Fraulein,*" Magara said, "but it seems a pity."

Theola did not listen.

She was taking from one of the drawers the heavy lace veil that Catherine had brought with her to wear on her wedding-day.

It was to have been held in place by a diamond tiara which the Duchess had entrusted to her daughter at the last moment.

But Catherine had not taken it with her, in fact she must have forgotten it. But in any case, Theola knew that the tiara would look heavy and too over-opulent on her.

She was not particularly enamoured of the lace veil, either. It was beautiful lace, but she felt it was somehow overpowering.

"I have an idea, Magara!" she said suddenly, and pulled open the drawer at the bottom of the wardrobe.

With her usual mania for economy, the Duchess had included in Catherine's luggage several rolls of material with which to repair her gowns.

"You understand, Theola," she had said, "that when the trains of Catherine's dresses become torn or dirty you are to sew new frills onto them several times before they are discarded."

"Yes, Aunt Adelaide."

"You can sew well when you want to," the Duchess said sharply, "and therefore I shall instruct Catherine to see that you perform this task as soon as the necessity arises."

The Duchess had then shown Theola the rolls of extra material and told her several times over how carefully she was to do the repairs.

Now Theola fetched a roll of tulle from the drawer and put it beside the gown on the bed.

When she was dressed in the wedding-gown, which Magara had altered for her, she could hardly recognise her own reflection in the mirror.

Never before had she realised what a tiny waist she had or how exquisitely her small breasts curved above it.

Her neck and shoulders were dazzlingly white and the gown, now that the unnecessary flowers and glittering ribbons had been removed, made her look very young, innocent, and pure.

With the long train rippling behind her she was indeed like a "nymph from the foam."

Instead of the heavy veil, she showed Magara how to make one from the tulle and to hold it in place with a simple wreath of orange-blossom from which Theola had removed the diamanté.

"You look beautiful, *Fraulein!*" Magara said with a note of awe in her voice when Theola was finally ready. "You look like a bride, and at the same time you look like one of the statues of the Saints in the Cathedral."

'That is how I want to look,' Theola thought, but she did not say so aloud.

When she was told that the General was waiting
for her she walked slowly along the wide corridor,
hearing for the first time in her life the silken swish of
a train moving behind her.

She reached the Grand Staircase, and as she put out
her hand towards the banisters she saw that the General was waiting for her in the Hall below.

He was wearing the green uniform of the Kavōnian
Army, but now on his tunic there were epaulettes, and
the red ribbon of a Religious Order hung at his side.

He watched Theola as she came down the stairs.

As she reached him and looked up into his eyes she
saw in them an expression she had hoped to see,
which was very different from the contempt with
which he had once regarded her.

He looked at her for a long moment, then raised
her white-gloved hand to his lips.

"You look exactly as I expected you would," he said
quietly, and she hoped that meant he thought her
beautiful.

There was a small bouquet of white roses which
Magara gave into her hand at the last moment.

Theola saw that there was an open carriage waiting outside the Palace door. It was decorated with
flowers and the horses drawing it had flowers round
their necks and on their bridles.

They drove slowly down the long, broad road which
led to the Square.

As they reached it, Theola saw that it was thronged
with people, packed tightly, as it had been when
Catherine had arrived, but somehow now there was
a difference.

At first she could not explain it to herself. The
cheers rang out whole-heartedly and everyone seemed
to be smiling.

She stepped from the carriage and saw that in the
very centre of the Square was a platform and on it
was the Mayor, resplendent in red robes with a gold
chain round his neck.

Between the carriage and the platform it was only a short walk over a carpet which had been laid in the roadway, and as the General gave Theola his arm the people on either side went down on their knees.

For a moment Theola could hardly believe it was happening.

Then she knew the difference between the cheers she had heard today and those when Catherine had arrived. There was a reverence in the voices that had not been there before.

They reached the platform and for the first time since she had left the Palace Theola suddenly felt nervous.

Perhaps her hand on his arm trembled, perhaps he was perceptive enough to know what she was feeling, but the General turned and smiled at her.

"You are giving my people faith and hope," he said in a low voice that only she could hear.

He could have said nothing to sweep away her nervousness more effectively, and now she no longer thought of herself but of the people.

They stood in front of the Mayor and he greeted them with a short address in Kavōnian.

He told the General how the people looked to him to lead them, as his family had done for centuries, and how the hearts of everyone were with him on this, the happiest day of his life.

All the time he was speaking, the vast throng of people in the Square was completely silent.

"We require your signature, General," the Mayor said to Alexius Vasilas.

"I thought we had to take our vows in front of you," the General replied.

"I have wonderful news for you," the Mayor replied. "When you announced this morning that I would marry you, a message was sent to the Monastery and the Archbishop has returned to the city!"

Theola felt the General stiffen and before the Mayor continued she knew what he was about to say.

"You will be married in the Cathedral, as I know you would wish to be. The Archbishop is waiting for you now."

Theola felt that Alexius Vasilas was turned to stone and she herself found it hard to breathe.

Then automatically the General signed his name in the Civil Marriage Register and Theola added hers with stiff fingers.

The Mayor turned towards the silent people.

"My children," he said, "Alexius Vasilas, who has returned to rule over us and who has just been joined in marriage according to the law of Kavōnia, will now be married according to our faith and the faith of our ancestors.

"Our beloved Archbishop is waiting in the Cathedral and the bride and bridegroom will now go there to receive the blessing of God upon their union."

There was a wild cheer of delight which seemed to echo into the sky itself.

Then Theola, holding on to the General's arm, found herself being led to the other side of the platform and along a carpet which had been laid to the very door of the Cathedral which stood at the far end of the Square.

As they began their walk, the people kneeling on either side of them, the General said:

"Forgive me! This is not what I had planned, but there is nothing I can do about it at this moment."

"No, of course not," Theola agreed.

It was impossible to say any more, and they moved slowly and with dignity through the cheering throng until they reached the Cathedral where a number of Priests were waiting for them.

Theola had never been inside a Greek Orthodox Church, but her father had described it to her and now the hanging silver lamps, the profusion of candles, and the scent of incense seemed somehow familiar.

As they walked up the aisle the people surged into the Cathedral behind them and Theola thought how different it would have looked if it had been filled with Austrians in their luxurious gowns, the Court dignitaries in red and gold covered with glittering decorations.

The Archbishop in his black robes was waiting for them and voices clear and lovely filled the Cathedral with melody.

When she handed her bouquet to one of those who were officiating, she also removed her gloves.

Because she was feeling nervous and very afraid of doing the wrong thing, she instinctively put her hand into the General's, as a child might have done.

She felt his fingers tighten on hers and somehow they were as comforting as his arms had been when he had carried her upstairs after the soldier had assaulted her.

The Service was very beautiful and the Greek in which it was spoken made her think of her father and long for him to be present.

She wondered if he knew she was being married and in such strange circumstances.

Somehow she felt he did and that he was near her and approved of what she was doing.

Wreaths of flowers and ribbon linked together were blessed by the Archbishop and placed on the General's head and hers. Then their hands were joined and she felt him put a ring on her finger.

The Archbishop's voice was very solemn as he made the sign of the cross and blessed them. Then an organ blared forth a march and they proceeded down the aisle towards the sunshine coming through the West Door.

The cheers of the crowds made it impossible for them to speak as they drove away from the Cathedral, and now flowers were thrown into the carriage until they were covered with a sweet-scented blanket of blossom.

Only when they reached the Court-Yard of the Palace was there comparative quiet, and for the first time since they had been married Theola turned her face towards the General.

He was looking at her, she found, and there was an expression in his eyes which she did not understand.

"I promise you," he said in his deep voice, "that I had no idea the Archbishop might return to Zanthos for our wedding."

Theola did not speak and after a moment he said:

"Because you are not of the same Church as I am, there will, I am sure, be ways of annulling the marriage later."

They had reached the steps of the Palace before Theola could reply to him.

Here the staff were all assembled, looking very unlike the resplendent guests who had been waiting for Catherine, but there was no mistaking the sincerity of their congratulations, which came from the very depths of their hearts.

"Thank you! Thank you!" the General said as they spoke to him.

Several of the women knelt to kiss Theola's hands as she walked up the steps and others raised the hem of her gown to their lips.

They reached the Hall and the General turned to Theola.

"I know you will understand that there is a great deal for me to do before we leave the city. Will you be ready at eight o'clock, wearing riding-clothes? Until then, I suggest it would be wise for you to rest."

"Yes, of course," Theola answered.

He raised her hand to his lips and she had a strange impulse to hold on to him, not to let him go.

But a second later he had left her and Theola walked alone up the staircase with only Magara beside her.

* * *

It was not yet dark as they left the city, but the sun was sinking in a blaze of crimson and gold behind the mountains.

There was no cheering as the soldiers left, only

shouts of "Good luck!" "God bless you and bring you back safely!"

Some of the women were weeping as they said good-bye to their husbands and sons.

The soldiers did not move in smart, orderly ranks, such as the Austrians would have expected, but were talking to one another without formation.

The General was riding with Theola beside him and several other officers were on horse-back, but the majority were on foot, walking with their men, chatting with them on equal terms.

Theola thought what a contrast it was to the stiff, almost-insolent aloofness of the Austrian officers.

She was wearing a riding-habit belonging to Catherine because her own was so old and dilapidated that she would have been ashamed for the people to see her in it.

It was in fact a summer habit of very pale pink frogged with white braid and really quite unsuitable for a war-like expedition.

But if she was to be a symbol not only to the people but also to the Army, Theola thought, she had to look the part.

She noticed that when she appeared the soldiers looked at her appreciatively, but at the same time with respect, and she knew her appearance was what they would have wished.

She was not certain what the General felt, for he had had no time to speak to her and was busy giving orders and instructions up to the very last moment.

The city, she learnt, was filling up with people and the population was increasing hour by hour.

When they left, not only the market-place but also the Square in which they had been married was full of sheep, cattle, and goats, all protesting vocally at their unaccustomed surroundings.

The noise was as awesome as it had been at the moment at which they had mounted the platform for the Civil Ceremony.

Theola had the feeling that the General was rather embarrassed at what had occurred and was still not quite certain how to cope with it.

She did not have to be told that he was a very religious man. She knew it instinctively.

She was aware, as they had knelt before the Archbishop in front of the beautiful silver altar, that a reverence and a feeling of sanctity came from him which was unmistakable.

"How could we ever be free after being married in such circumstances?" Theola asked herself.

She wondered whether it was disturbing him at this moment when he should be thinking only of the fight which lay ahead with the King's forces.

Darkness came swiftly as the sun sank, but there was a half-moon in the sky and the stars were soon brilliant above the high peaks of the mountains.

It grew cold and Theola was glad to avail herself of the heavy Cavalry-cloak lined with sheepskin which Magara had insisted should be laid at the back of her saddle, ready for when she should require it.

When they paused at the foot of the mountains an officer came to her side to unfasten it from her saddle.

As he did so she saw to her surprise and delight that it was Captain Petlos!

"You are with us!" she exclaimed impulsively. "I am so glad!"

"Could I be anywhere else?" he asked with a smile. "I have wanted to have an opportunity to talk to you ever since I have been in Zanthos."

"I had a great deal to do for the General."

"You were in touch with him all the time you were in the Palace?" she asked.

"Alexius Vasilas persuaded me that I could serve him best by being there."

"I can understand that," Theola replied.

He placed the cloak over her shoulders, and as he did so a soldier came up to him and said:

"The General wishes to speak to you, Major."

"Major!" Theola exclaimed.

"I have been promoted," he explained, "and I do not mind telling you that I consider I deserve it after what I have had to put up with these last few years!"

He smiled as he spoke. Then he was gone from her side and she sat waiting for the order to move on.

It was an hour later when Theola found herself in a cave halfway up the mountains.

It smelt slightly of some wild animal, but it was clean and had a sandy floor.

She realised that from it she could look down onto the road winding through the valley below, the road along which the King's Army must travel to reach Zanthos.

All along the mountains there were caves, gorges, jagged rocks, and chasms in which men could be concealed without anyone having the slightest idea they were there.

The cave into which she had been escorted was large, and a soldier placed a blanket on the floor on which she could sit and arranged another one against the opposite wall of the cave.

"Is that for the General?" Theola enquired.

"Yes, Your Excellency," the soldier answered.

He put a telescope and several other objects down on the other blanket, saluted, and left Theola alone.

She took off her cloak, sat down on the blanket, and waited.

It was not yet midnight, and she knew it would be impossible to rest when she felt so tense and so apprehensive about what the morning would bring.

She was sure that the General was seeing his men into position on the other side of the valley and she hardly expected that he would come to the cave at all.

Yet, at about two o'clock, when the moon was no longer high in the sky, he suddenly appeared.

"Are you all right?" he asked.

"I was worrying about you."

"I have done everything I can do," the General said, sitting down on the blanket. "All our men are in position, and it would be a mistake for anyone to move about now in case the enemy send scouts ahead who might discover where we are."

"That sounds sensible," Theola remarked.

"I have something for you," he said.

"What is it?"

"A pistol! I think you should be armed. Do you know how to fire one?"

"Yes, I do," Theola replied. "I used to fire an old duelling-pistol, which my father inherited from his grand-father, at a target in the garden."

"I hope you will never have to use this," the General said, "but just in case things go wrong it is wise to have one with you."

He held it out to Theola as he spoke and she took it from him.

As she did so she thought quite calmly and unemotionally that if things did "go wrong," as he put it, she might have to use the pistol on herself.

"It is loaded," the General said warningly.

"I will be very careful," Theola said.

She put it down on the blanket.

"I suggest, Theola, that you try to sleep," the General said. "That is what I intend to do. Tomorrow will undoubtedly be a hard day."

"You must certainly sleep," Theola answered. "Everything depends on you, as you well know."

"I thought that today when we were being married," the General said.

He paused, then added:

"I do not need to tell you how wonderful you were and what it meant to the people to believe that you had come to their aid in the most crucial moment of their lives."

There was a note in his voice that made Theola feel as if she vibrated to music.

"Thank you," she said.

The General lay back on the blanket.

"Good-night, Theola!" he said in a very different tone of voice.

She wanted to ask him not to sleep, to go on talking to her. There was so much she wanted to know, so much she wanted to hear.

Then she knew that it was imperative that he should rest.

He had been working all day, and now if he could sleep for a short time he would be ready to lead his Army in what he had rightly said was the most crucial moment of their lives.

"Oh, God, let him win!" Theola prayed.

Instead of lying on her back, she lay face downwards so that she could look out of the cave and into the moonlight, and raise her eyes to the snow-capped peaks towering above them.

She felt as if they pointed the way to Heaven, or was it at the gods in which her father had believed?

Perhaps the gods would be with them tomorrow, and the spirits which dwelt in the mountains and in the cascades tumbling down their sides would rally behind them to bring the Kavōnians peace and happiness.

Theola was not sleepy. She wanted to go on praying, because she felt it was so important that her prayers should be heard.

"Help us, Papa," she prayed to her father. "Show the General what is the right thing to do. Help him to conquer his enemies."

It was very quiet and the beauty and peace of the night belonged to another world.

Theola felt herself so caught up in the magic of it that she no longer remembered the men crouching with their weapons and waiting in ambush.

She knew now that the General was sleeping peacefully and dreamlessly as only a soldier can sleep in a moment of relaxation.

She could hear his even breathing and she wished it were not so dark, so that she could look at him and see his perfect features when his eyes were closed.

She was thinking of him as Apollo when suddenly she became aware of a soft movement.

She thought it was an animal moving amongst the rocks and had a little stab of fear that it might be a snake.

Then, incredulously, she saw the head of a man!

He was moving just below the cave and now as she looked down she realised that he was crawling through some rocks, moving higher as he did so, and edging himself almost silently towards the cave itself.

It flashed through her mind that it must be a soldier bringing the General a message and not wishing to be seen by the enemy scouts.

She wondered whether she should awaken the General and tell him that the man needed him. Then, as she hesitated, the man raised himself a little further and she saw that in his hand he was carrying a long, pointed knife!

It glittered in the light from the moon and as she looked at it she knew this was no messenger but an assailant!

Without thinking, instinctively she put her hand down on the blanket and grasped the pistol which the General had given to her.

The man raised himself a little further and now he was at the very mouth of the cave and Theola saw the knife flash as he raised it in his hand.

She fired and the report echoed and re-echoed in the cave, and even as the General sat up the assailant toppled over backwards and rolled slowly, a number of stones travelling with him, down the side of the mountain.

"What has happened? Why did you shoot?" the General demanded.

Then he saw just inside the cave on a ledge of rock the knife which the man had held in his hand.

In the light of the moon it looked evil and there was no need for Theola to make any explanations.

The General climbed down the side of the mountain to where the man lay.

Theola heard soldiers talking to him.

She sat trembling, and yet killing a man was not the

emotional horror she had expected it to be. Instead, she felt somehow detached, as if it were something which had happened outside herself.

The General came back.

As he entered the cave he picked up Theola's pistol from where she had laid it and started to reload it.

"You saved my life!" he said quietly.

"Who . . . was that . . . man?" Theola enquired.

"He was a scout for the King's Army," the General said briefly.

"Do you think they now know you are here?" Theola asked in a frightened voice.

"I doubt it," he replied. "I think the man saw us arrive. Instead of reporting to his base, as he should have done, he thought he would be clever and claim the reward that has been offered for my life."

"Then you will still be able to surprise them?" Theola asked.

"I hope so," the General answered, "and once again, thank you!"

He spoke calmly, as if he was determined the moment should not be emotional. And because she felt he expected it of her, Theola lay down and shut her eyes. As she did so the words of the legend came to her mind.

"The nymph would save the light from the darkness."

If she was the nymph, then the light of Kavōnia was undoubtedly Alexius Vasilas, and she had saved him from the darkness of death and perhaps the Kavōnians themselves from the darkness of the enemy.

CHAPTER FIVE

Theola knew that the General was not asleep.

He did not speak and he kept very still, and yet she knew instinctively that he was awake.

She thought perhaps he was listening in case the shot with which she had killed his assailant had alerted the enemy forces.

Then she reasoned to herself that the report from her pistol would not have carried far, and if there was only one scout there was no reason to think that anyone except their own troops would have heard it.

But she could understand the General being tense and anxious lest his plans should go wrong. She wanted to talk to him, wanted him to reassure her that she had done the right thing.

She had killed a man!

There was nothing else she could have done! And Theola was sure that the General was right when he'd said the scout must have seen them arrive and hoped to gain for himself the prize money the King had offered for Alexius Vasilas, dead or alive.

If he had been successful in killing the General, Theola knew, the revolution would have failed.

The King would have come back to treat the people with even more severity than he had in the past.

Now that she understood how harsh King Ferdinand's rule had been, it seemed incredible that he had lasted on the throne for so long.

But he had been wise enough to protect himself and his Austrian friends with weapons which could stamp out an insurrection almost as soon as it arose.

Men with empty hands, however resolute their hearts might be, were helpless against the modern weapons of war.

Theola could understand that it had taken years of planning before Alexius Vasilas could be sure he was at last strong enough to challenge the all-powerful Austrians.

The moon moved higher up the sky and now with its light and the brilliance of the stars Theola could see the outline of the General as he lay on the other side of the cave.

She had a feeling that although he was in darkness there was a light about him. A light which must guide and lead his people once he had defeated their enemies.

"Help him, God . . . please help him," Theola prayed, "and . . . forgive me for having . . . taken a man's life."

She had often thought that if she killed anyone she would be overcome with guilt and remorse.

When the General killed the soldier who had assaulted her, she had felt only relief; and now, instead of feeling ashamed of having killed the scout, she was glad, because it meant the General was alive.

It seemed incredible that only a few weeks ago she was in England, miserable, crushed, and unhappy, frightened even to speak in case she should say the wrong thing, facing a life-sentence of drudgery from which there seemed to be no chance of escape.

Now she was here on the side of a mountain beside a man who was fighting a "life or death" battle for the freedom of his country.

"And I am . . . married to him!" Theola whispered beneath her breath.

She was well aware that while Alexius Vasilas might find it easy to dissolve a Civil Marriage, it was going to be far more difficult for him to rid himself of a wife whom he had married according to the sacraments of his Church.

Theola knew very little about religious laws, but she was sure that the Service in which she had taken part was insolubly binding and that as far as the Archbishop was concerned they would remain man and wife until they were parted by death.

'There must be some form of annulment, perhaps because I am of a different faith,' she thought.

Then her heart asked:

"What will become of you?"

She could hardly bear to contemplate the only alternative if she had to leave Kavōnia, and deliberately she forced herself to think of their situation at the moment.

She turned over once again to look out of the cave. She saw the mountains opposite.

The moonlight was shining on the snow-capped peaks, which, silhouetted against the star-strewn sky, were exquisitely beautiful.

It was easy to believe as she looked at them that the spirits of the mountains were supernatural and far above the petty strivings of human beings.

"Help us! Help us!" Theola found herself whispering, and wondered if in fact there were such forces who would range themselves on the side of freedom and humanity tomorrow.

She must have dozed a little. Then she heard the General stir and knew it must be nearly dawn.

She thought there was a faint light in the East and the stars were not as bright as they had been.

"What are you going to do?" she asked in a whisper.

They were the first words she had spoken since he had thanked her for saving his life.

"I am going to make sure that everyone is on the alert," he replied.

"Do you think they will . . . come early?"

"I imagine they will start to move at dawn," the General replied. "That is what I should do if I were in their position."

"Will there be . . . many of . . . them?" Theola asked, a little tremor in her voice.

"I am not afraid of their numbers," the General replied, "but of their guns! If, as I have heard, they have long-range guns, then we have to stop them before they can bombard Zanthos."

Theola felt a little shiver run through her.

She knew the city was not built to withstand a bombardment, and the fact that so many people were congregated in it made it seem even more vulnerable.

She had not understood this policy and could not help asking:

"Why did you draw so many people into the city? Surely it means that far more are likely to be injured?"

She knew that in the darkness the General looked at her sharply, as if he was surprised at her question.

Then he answered her quietly and seriously, saying:

"If the King's forces pass through this valley and get a foothold, they will send marauding bands to kill the peasants in the outlying villages and carry off their flocks. An Army is always hungry and I do not imagine the King has found large stocks of food waiting for him at the border."

"No, of course not," Theola agreed. "Now I understand."

"It is unusual for a woman to wish to comprehend the manoeuvrings of Armies," the General said.

"I am interested only in *your* Army," Theola replied, "but I hate to think of the suffering this battle will inflict upon so many human beings wherever they have placed their allegiance."

"That is why I believe that by ambushing the enemy troops here, we shall, if we are successful, save immeasurable suffering."

"I have prayed that you will win," Theola said quietly. "I have been praying all night, and I think you have too."

It was something, she thought to herself, that she could not have said to the General if they had been in the daylight.

But it was easy to talk to him when he was only a shadowy figure on the other side of the cave.

"I am sure your prayers will be answered," he replied, "and may I tell you once again how grateful I am, not only that you saved my life, but also because you have been brave enough to come with us."

"I think the truth is," Theola said, "I was not brave enough to stay behind."

"It is not the way most women would look at the situation," he answered.

"Do you . . . think the men are . . . glad I am . . . here?" Theola asked hesitatingly.

She hoped he would not think it a conceited question.

"I believe every man will fight as he has never fought before and will in his heart believe we will be victorious!"

The General spoke with a note of sincerity in his voice that was unmistakable and after a moment Theola said:

"Thank you for . . . telling me . . . that."

"I thought when I saw you riding with us yesterday," the General said, "you looked like Joan of Arc following the inspiration of her 'voices,' which put new strength and new life into the wavering French."

"That is what I . . . want to do," Theola said. "But I am . . . afraid that I may fail."

"How could you do that when up to now you have been so magnificent?" the General asked. "You might have refused when I asked you to marry me, and I never dreamt that you would accompany me to the forefront of the battle."

He rose as he spoke and now Theola realised that while they had been talking the first fingers of the sun were creeping up the sky.

She, too, rose to stand beside him, looking out on the mountains on either side of the valley.

There was not a movement to be seen. The place looked utterly desolate—and yet there were hundreds of men waiting there, priming their weapons, ready to kill or be killed for the sake of the future.

"Must you . . . go now?" Theola asked.

"You are to stay here," the General said with a note of authority in his voice. "There are two men whom I would trust with my own life on either side of you, and if by any chance things do go wrong you can trust them to take you to safety."

Theola knew exactly what he meant by saying "if things go wrong." He meant that if he himself was killed.

She felt her heart give a frightened leap. Then impulsively she moved nearer to him.

"You will be careful?" she begged. "Promise me you will be very careful and take no chances with yourself."

He did not answer and after a moment she went on:

"You must be aware that without you everything will fail. The whole future of Kavōnia depends on your remaining alive."

"Do we in this small, unimportant country matter so much to you?" the General asked.

"Of course you do!" Theola answered. "I am now a part of you, so please . . . please be careful."

She raised her face to his as she pleaded with him.

Then suddenly, so unexpectedly that she gave a little cry, he pulled her roughly into his arms.

His lips took possession of hers.

For a moment she was too astonished to feel anything except that his mouth was hard and possessive.

Then something wild and wonderful flashed through her body like a streak of light.

She had never known it possible that she could feel anything so rapturous, so intensely glorious, that it was beyond description.

The General's arms tightened until she could hardly breathe and she felt he had captured not only her lips but her whole body.

He swept her towards the stars and a blinding light enveloped them both.

'This is the glory of the gods,' Theola thought.

She felt that her heart had passed into his keeping and she was no longer herself but a part of him.

As suddenly as he had taken her he released her, and turning, he left the cave. She heard him moving down the side of the mountain.

For a moment she could only feel as if her legs were giving way under her and it was hard not to fall to the ground.

Her whole being throbbed with the ecstasy he had evoked in her. On her lips she could still feel the hard pressure of his, and the light of the gods was still in her eyes.

Hardly aware of what she was doing, she sat down on the blanket, her hands going to her breasts as if she would still the tumult in them.

She knew that she loved him, and she had never known, never imagined, that love would be like this.

She had always thought that it was something warm, happy, and comfortable, like the love she had seen between her father and mother.

But this was different. This was wild and passionate . . . a burning fire that seemed to ripple through her like flames seering their way into her consciousness.

"I . . . love him! I love . . . him!"

She knew now that she must have loved him when he was carrying her upstairs after she had been assaulted by the soldier, and she had felt the security and protection of his arms.

It was something she had not experienced since her father and mother had died—to feel safe and unafraid.

Even after all she had been through and the terror the drunken soldier had evoked in her, she had known, too, although she was unable to express it herself, that Alexius Vasilas had meant something very special—something which was different from anything she had ever encountered in her life before.

"It is love," Theola told herself, and wondered why she had not realised it before.

It was love that had made her long for him to come and talk to her; it was love, although she had had no idea of it, when he had asked her to be his wife and she had agreed.

He had said it was to protect her and to make the legend in which the Kavōnian people believed come true.

Thinking back, she was certain that if any other man had asked her to do the same thing she would have been apprehensive and very reluctant to agree to the suggestion.

But she had been only too willing to entrust herself to the General and do anything he suggested.

She had loved him.

"I saved his life!" she told herself. "I saved him! It was not only for the sake of Kavōnia but also because if he had died I would have died too."

She heard a sudden sound and raised her head to see that the sable of the night was receding and the stars had vanished.

Now the dawn was rising behind the mountains and on the other side of the valley the peaks had turned from silver in the moonlight to a dazzling iridescence against the morning sky.

The noise which Theola had heard seemed to have

come from the valley and now she looked down and could see the winding road quite clearly.

The night before, she had not noticed that there was a stream running beside it, rocky and not very wide or deep at this time of year, but in the winter it would be swollen by the cascades coming down from the snows.

The road was empty and there was nothing to be seen, and yet the sound was growing louder and Theola realised with a little tremor of fear that it was the noise of marching feet.

She knew that every man commanded by Alexius Vasilas would have heard, as she had, the approaching enemy and would be alert, their weapons ready, waiting only for the order to fire.

This, Theola knew, would be given by the General, and she wished that she knew where he was and could see him.

Surely after what she had said to him he would not do anything foolhardy or deliberately take any risks?

He must understand that only by remaining alive could he help his people.

If he was dead they would be left without a leader and without inspiration.

"He must be careful! He must!" she told herself frantically.

She had pleaded with him before to take care, but now that she admitted to herself that she loved him, it was an inexpressible agony to think that he was in danger.

Perhaps he would be struck by a stray bullet or killed in direct combat, because every man in the King's Army would be aware, as she was, that if they killed Vasilas the revolution would be over.

The sound of tramping feet, which came from the South of the valley, was getting louder, and now as Theola watched she saw the first soldiers come into sight.

The light was getting clearer every second and she could see an officer on horse-back flanked by two of the King's personal bodyguard, their helmets, which had reminded her of Greek Warriors', glinting in the rays of the sun.

Behind them came guns, the heavy, long-range guns which Alexius Vasilas feared and which Theola knew could bombard Zanthos into a pitiable ruin.

They each were drawn by four mules, and as the column came slowly along the winding road she saw that there were eight of them. Eight heavy guns, their crews marching behind them, six men to each gun.

Behind the guns came more officers in their smart red tunics, leading men marching smartly in formation, very unlike the casual and friendly rabble commanded by Alexius Vasilas.

It was impossible at this distance for Theola to see their rifles clearly, but she was sure they were the latest, up-to-date, quick-firing models, and she thought despairingly of the ancient flint-locks she had seen being carried by their own men.

"How can we ever succeed against such formidable odds?" she asked herself anxiously.

She clenched her hands together, feeling that only prayer and the faith of the People's Army could help them now.

The officer leading the guns was halfway through the valley and still there were soldiers behind him who had not yet entered it.

Theola thought there must be hundreds of them and imagined that more mercenaries than the General had anticipated must have joined the King's forces, if not from Kavōnia then from Greece.

On and on they marched, moving at an even pace, the guns rumbling over the rocky track, the soldiers occasionally beating the mules. But otherwise, except for the sound of marching feet, there was silence.

There were no sharp commands, no voice was raised, there was just the rumble of wheels and the sounds of horses' hoofs and marching feet.

It was uncanny and at the same time awe-inspiring.

So many of them! So regimented! So precise!

Soldiers who had been drilled and trained to kill. Soldiers who were professionals.

Theola had the idea that there were not many Kavōnians among them, although of course she could not be sure.

The General had said that most of the Kavōnian Army had defected to him, and she knew that there were many professional soldiers amongst those hidden on either side of the valley.

But there was also a large number of ordinary citizens who were simply followers of Alexius Vasilas and had had no military training except for what little he might have been able to give them.

They would be likely to feel overwhelmed by the might of the King's forces.

"I am . . . afraid," Theola told herself.

She wondered if perhaps the men hiding behind the rocks and in the caves and gorges might not suddenly throw away their arms and run rather than risk losing their lives.

She could hardly believe that they would desert their leader, especially as it was Alexius Vasilas.

But who could be sure how a man untrained and untried would react when it came to the moment when he must risk the only precious thing he possessed—his life?

"Give them courage! Oh, God, give them courage!" Theola prayed, and realised that the officer leading the guns had almost reached the open end of the valley.

Now she could see that the last of the King's forces had appeared and below her was a long crocodile of uniformed men moving precisely and with measured tread, filling the whole road of the valley.

It was indeed an awe-inspiring sight, and had it not been for the hidden Kavōnians, Theola thought with a kind of sick horror, Alexius Vasilas might have changed his mind.

Perhaps he had decided that the position was hopeless; perhaps after all he would not risk the lives of his own people and would surrender to the King.

Even as the thought made her tremble there was a sudden explosion.

A shot rang out and as it echoed and re-echoed in the mountains, the leading officer fell from his horse while the animal galloped away unharmed.

It was the signal for a general fusilade from both sides of the valley.

Alexius Vasilas's men were firing from behind the rocks, from the caves, from the gorges, and from the chasms. The precise formation of the troops below disintegrated as the soldiers ran to find cover at the sides of the road.

Only the mules pulling the guns carried on along the roadway, quickening their pace and plunging about in terror at the noise of the gun-fire.

Now there were a few answering shots, but only a few.

The men taking cover by the side of the stream were pointing their rifles at the rocks looming above them, but it was almost impossible for them to find a clear target.

Their bullets ricocheted off the barren stones, doing little harm.

The noise was overwhelming not only from the rifles themselves but also from the reverberation in the valley.

Every shot echoed and re-echoed in the caves and among the mountains, being magnified until the sound of it seemed to pound on the ears.

Now all the King's men were lying down or crouching behind boulders until, as the cross-fire took terrible toll of their numbers, they started to run.

It was the gunners who ran first, because they had no personal weapons, and as they tore back over the road they were joined by others, throwing away their rifles as if they impeded their progress. Some of them even discarded their tunics so that they could run faster.

So quickly that it was difficult to realise it had actually happened, the gunners had started a rout that was almost pitiable.

Stricken with terror, men ran, forgetting everything but the need for self-preservation. Those who remained behind were no longer firing, because they were dead.

Theola could see one or two officers trying to stem the tide, but it was hopeless.

Those who still had horses galloped away, and the others ran as swiftly as they could after them.

Then, as she watched, Theola saw their own fighters coming out of their hiding-places and climbing down into the valley.

She saw the General giving orders and the men hurrying to obey him, and cheering as they did so.

They were cheering what she knew was an overwhelming victory. It was such an unutterable relief after the tension that she found tears running down her face and it was difficult to see any more.

* * *

It was a long time later that Major Petlos came to tell her that he had come to escort her from the cave and the General was waiting for her.

He was looking, Theola thought, exceedingly happy, although his smart uniform was covered with dust. There was a long scratch on his cheek and the finger of one hand was bleeding.

"You are hurt!" she exclaimed.

"Entirely through my own fault," he answered. "I was scrambling too quickly amongst the rocks in the excitement of getting down to the road."

"We won!" Theola said breathlessly.

"A magnificent victory!" Major Petlos said, his eyes shining. "And who could have done it but the General?"

"Have there been many casualties on our side?" Theola asked.

"Practically none!" the Major answered. "A few men are wounded and those who were killed exposed themselves unnecessarily."

He gave a deep sigh.

"Only the General could have been clever enough not only to plan how we could defeat the enemy, but also to make our men hold their fire until the very last minute."

He gave a laugh.

"It was not easy. Those who were not trained soldiers were longing to shoot on sight. It was only because they were afraid to disobey the General that we were able to keep them under control."

Theola had put on her hat while she was waiting, and now she brushed the sand from her skirt and held out her gloved hand to Major Petlos so that he could help her down the mountainside.

"You are amazing!" he said. "You look, Ma'am, as if you had just stepped out of a band-box, and I am sure the men will think it is all part of your supernatural origin."

"I am so glad that I was here," Theola said. "I think I would have gone mad if I had had to wait in Zanthos, not knowing what was happening."

If she was glad she had been with the fighting forces, there was no doubt as she proceeded down the mountainside that they were proud she had been with them.

The majority of the men were gathered round the guns, looking at them with awe and realising that in capturing from the King's Army their most formidable weapons, they had ensured that there would be no chance of any retaliation.

A number of other men were collecting the rifles which had been thrown away by the retreating Army. Others were tending to those of the enemy who were wounded but alive, and making them as comfortable as they could.

"Tell them," Theola heard the General say, "that we will send vehicles to bring them to Zanthos where a doctor will attend to them."

His voice rang out above the noise of everyone talking excitedly.

Then as Theola came down the last incline before she reached the road, the soldiers turned and saw her. A great cheer went up so spontaneously, and was so heartfelt, that once again she felt tears come to her eyes.

The General saw why they were cheering and turned towards Theola and Major Petlos, but he could not reach them.

Having cheered, the soldiers surrounded Theola and went down on one knee to kiss her hands.

She felt shy at their homage and yet there was nothing she could do but smile and thank them in their own language.

She felt a little strange as they pulled their caps from their heads and she felt their lips on her hands.

There seemed to be a great number who wished to pay her homage.

When she felt that perhaps she was delaying them from carrying out the General's orders, she looked towards him and realised he was watching her with a strange expression in his eyes.

She could not determine if he was pleased or annoyed, but a moment later Major Petlos led her to her horse and lifted her into the saddle.

"They have canonised you already," he said in a low voice. "I hope, Ma'am, you will enjoy being a Saint!"

She felt he was trying to relieve her tension and she smiled at him; but it was difficult to speak because she was in fact so deeply moved by the soldiers' actions.

The General, having given out orders, signalled to Theola to come to his side and together they rode ahead of the long column of men and guns on their way back to Zanthos.

She knew it was a deliberate show of strength, to

give the people of the city confidence and also to give them a chance to acclaim the men who had saved them from devastation by the King's forces.

As they rode, Theola kept glancing at the General, hoping he would talk to her.

There was, however, no chance of private conversation since at every moment it seemed that someone wanted to ask him a question or else he had to give an order which necessitated his riding back along the line of men to speak to one of the officers who were watching the progress of the guns.

Long before they reached Zanthos, Theola realised that the news of the victory had already reached the city.

They could see crowds of people coming out to meet them and flags were flying on the houses.

The cheers, throwing of flowers, and wild rejoicing among the people exceeded anything Theola could ever have imagined.

As they rode into the Square the children threw flowers in front of their horses and the people's cries of welcome rang out while tears of happiness ran down the cheeks of the older women.

At times it was impossible for her and the General to proceed, since their horses could not make their way through the crowd.

Theola knew it was because so many of the women wanted to touch her, kiss the hem of her riding-habit, and fill her arms with flowers.

It was impossible for her to accept all she was given and at the same time hold the reins, so the flowers fell to the ground, only to be replaced by many more.

It seemed to Theola that it took hours before they reached the Palace, and even then the crowds which followed them streamed into the Court-Yard, pushing forward until they stopped only at the steps leading up to the front door.

The General dismounted and when Major Petlos, who was riding just behind them, helped Theola to the ground, he held out his hand to take hers, and led her up the steps to turn round at the top of them and face the people.

As far as Theola could see, there were multitudes filling the Court-Yard and the broad street that led back to the Square, climbing up onto the walls, up the trees, waving and shouting and cheering in a frenzied fashion that sounded like a very paean of thanks rising into the sky.

Theola waved until her arm ached. Then at last the General turned and led her into the Palace.

"You must be very tired," he said. "Go to your room and rest. I will arrange for some food to be sent to you immediately."

They were the first words he had spoken to her, Theola realised, since he had left her at dawn, but when she would have replied he turned away and instantly was surrounded by a group of officers seeking his instructions.

She went up the stairs knowing that she was in fact very tired, although she was still feeling elated by all that had happened.

Magara was waiting for her, and as Theola held out her hands to her the maid curtseyed and kissed them one after the other.

"We have won, Ma'am!" she said with tears in her eyes and a sob in her voice. "We are free, thanks to the General—and you!"

"Yes, we have won," Theola agreed, "but, Magara, I feel very dirty after sleeping all night in my clothes. I want a bath, and I think I should sleep for a little while."

"You must, Ma'am, for there will be a lot for you to do."

A bath was brought into the bed-room and water was poured into it from huge silver cans emblazoned with the King's Coat of Arms.

'They must mean an awful lot of work!' Theola thought automatically.

She relaxed in the warm scented water and felt her eyes closing with exhaustion.

She was in fact so tired that Magara helped her to dry herself and when she crept into bed she fell asleep instantly.

*　*　*

Theola awoke and realised her fatigue had passed and she felt invigorated, alert, and excited.

She touched the bell by the bed-side and immediately Magara appeared.

"I was just wondering whether I should awaken you, Ma'am," she said. "Do you realise that it is time to dress for dinner?"

"Is it as late as that?" Theola exclaimed in dismay. "How can I have slept for so long when there is so much I want to do, so much I want to hear?"

"The crowds are still outside," Magara said, "calling for you, and although the General has been forced to appear and wave to them several times, he refused to have you awakened."

"He must be tired too," Theola said.

Magara laughed.

"I doubt it, Ma'am! The General is noted for being tireless. Did nobody tell you about that?"

"Nobody!" Theola answered.

"Once when he was visiting his people among the mountains he found a little boy, the son of a shepherd, who had fallen into a gorge and injured his leg.

"He would have died if the General had not discovered him, and because the nearest doctor was many miles away he walked for three days and three nights, carrying the boy in his arms, until he could find the right man to attend to him!"

"How amazing!" Theola said.

Magara smiled.

"The General is amazing. He is not like other men, Ma'am—just as you are not like other ladies!"

"You must not say that," Theola said. "I am afraid I am very ordinary."

"No-one in Kavōnia will believe that after they saw you yesterday looking like the nymph of the legend and knew that you brought them victory."

"It was not I who gave them that," Theola said. "It was the General!"

"The General too," Magara agreed, "but I hear that if you had not saved his life there would have been no victory and nothing for us to celebrate."

Theola looked at her in surprise.

"How do you know that?"

"It was the General who told us," Magara replied. "When he stood on the steps of the Palace this afternoon and everyone was cheering him, he told them how it was all due to you that he was still alive."

Magara clasped her hands together.

"Oh, Ma'am, can you wonder we believe you are come from the gods to bring us happiness?"

Theola did not reply.

She was surprised that the General had told them what had occurred.

She thought that to explain the incident badly to the people might, perhaps, show that he was not as alert as he should have been, with the result that an enemy could approach so near to him that he might have been stabbed to death.

Instead, he had told the tale to make her a heroine and to enhance the feelings which the people already had about her.

She could not help wondering if possibly the General cared a little for her.

She had not dared to think even to herself that he might love her.

He had kissed her, but after all, what did that mean?

Any man going into battle would kiss good-bye the woman who was begging him to take care of himself.

Had he felt, as she had, that the kiss he had given her was so wonderful that it came from another world?

Had he too felt that they were both enveloped in

light? And had the fire which ran through her also burnt in him?

It was difficult for her to know: she had never been kissed before and had no idea what an ordinary kiss between a man and a woman should be.

She only knew that to her it had been a wonder beyond wonders and that she would never again be quite the same since it had happened.

The memory of it was like a precious jewel within her breast, or perhaps a better simile was the light of which her father had always spoken but which she had not quite understood until it had been ignited by the General's lips.

'I love him!' Theola thought. 'But he must never realise it if he does not love me!'

She could not help thinking that if in fact he loved her he would have spoken to her, or at least kissed her hand, before they started on the long ride back to Zanthos.

She had wanted him to say something as they rode ahead of the troops and when they faced the cheering crowds.

But while he had held her hand she had felt somehow that his mind was not on her but on the people who would accept him as their Ruler.

But surely it would have been easy for him to come up the stairs just for one word with her before she went to sleep?

Magara had asked her if she would like anything to eat or drink, but she was determined to wait until dinner, hoping she might dine alone with the General.

Now she was so anxious to see him that she had only one thought, and that was to be dressed quickly so that she would be ready if he sent for her or came to find her.

"What shall I wear, Magara?" she enquired.

"I have altered all the gowns to fit you, Ma'am."

"How could you have done that?" Theola asked.

"I have been working every minute—in fact all through the night, Ma'am!"

"Oh, Magara, how absurd of you! You must be so tired."

"How could I sleep thinking you might be in danger?" Magara asked.

Theola was very touched.

"You might have known I would be safe with the General."

"You might be safe with him, Ma'am, but he would not have been safe without you!"

That was true, Theola thought.

If she had not been awake or if she had lain down as he had and not looked out into the valley, the assailant could have entered the cave without either of them being aware of it.

"I think God has protected us both," she said aloud.

"There is to be a special Service of thanksgiving in the Cathedral the day after tomorrow," Magara said, "and people are asking how soon there will be a Coronation."

"A Coronation?" Theola ejaculated.

"Alexius Vasilas is the true heir to the throne!" Magara said. "His father reigned for fifteen years and his grand-father before him for twenty."

She paused, and then, seeing that Theola was interested, went on:

"The country was not completely united in those days as it is now, and there were Princes who claimed large territories and had their own Principalities."

"What has happened to them?" Theola asked.

"Most of them rebelled against King Ferdinand when he came to the throne and were either killed in battle or executed."

"And there are none left?" Theola asked.

"None of any importance, so Alexius Vasilas will be the King of the whole of Kavōnia."

Theola drew in her breath, knowing it was ridiculous to think for one moment that she might be Queen.

Catherine would have enjoyed the pomp and importance of wearing a crown and having a Court centred round her, but Theola knew it was not the sort of life she would like, and in fact was something for which she was not fitted.

For the first time she remembered that Alexius Vasilas knew nothing about her except that she was the niece of a Duke.

Her Uncle had said that she must never marry because of her mother's disgraceful action in mixing her noble blood with that of a common man.

Would Alexius Vasilas think that disgraceful?

He was a Prince—he was noble.

Theola had never thought of him like that before.

She always remembered how he had looked when he had come in his peasant-costume from the shuttered house to lift the wounded child into his arms.

His uniform was always without embellishment except for the Order he had worn when they were married.

And yet he was Royal! And of a dynasty perhaps as old, if not older, than King Ferdinand's.

'I must tell him,' she thought to herself, and felt herself shrinking from doing so because she was afraid of his reaction.

Meanwhile, Magara was still waiting for her to choose a gown.

There were so many in the wardrobe, all of them beautiful and quite unlike anything she had ever had the opportunity of wearing before.

Quite suddenly she felt shy and humble, and almost ashamed of herself.

How could she, who her Uncle had said was little better than a servant, be here in a Royal Palace, wear her cousin's trousseau, and deceive the hereditary Prince of Kavōnia into thinking she was someone of importance?

"Perhaps if he had known from the very beginning that I am not who I appear to be," she told herself unhappily, "he would not even have suggested that we should be married, even though it was in name only."

He had made quite clear to her that the Civil Mar-

126

riage could be terminated as soon as the war was over, but he had not then expected that they would be married in the Cathedral in accordance with the rites of the faith which was a part of his history.

"What can I do?" Theola asked herself.

She knew that to keep silent would only make things worse.

Sooner or later Alexius Vasilas would discover the truth about her.

She was quite certain that if no-one else informed him of it, her Uncle, if he should hear of their marriage, would undoubtedly make things as unpleasant as possible.

'He will denounce me!' she thought with a little shiver of fear.

Then she told herself that this, if nothing else, would be a justification for Alexius Vasilas to get their marriage dissolved.

"You must get dressed, Ma'am," Magara exclaimed, her voice breaking in on Theola's thoughts.

She realised she had been standing for a long time staring at Catherine's beautiful gowns, aware of nothing but her problem.

"Whichever you think the most suitable, Magara," she said.

"Yesterday, Ma'am, you wore white and looked like a Saint," Magara said. "Tonight I think you should look like a woman for your husband. That is what every man would want."

Theola did not answer and Magara lifted down from the wardrobe a gown of pale-pink gauze.

When she had it on Theola realised that nothing could be more becoming to her fair hair and the whiteness of her skin.

It made her look like a rose-bud, and there were in fact bunches of them embellishing the train and caught in front of the bodice where the folds of soft gauze encircled her bare shoulders.

Because she was so worried by her own anxieties, Theola hardly looked in the mirror as Magara arranged her hair and set a small posy of half-open roses amongst the curls at the back.

She was only just ready when there came a knock at the door.

Magara went to it, and came back into the room to say with a disappointed note in her voice:

"The General's compliments, Ma'am, but he is too busy to invite you to dine with him this evening. Instead he has sent your dinner here."

'It is what I might have expected,' Theola thought. 'I am of no further use to him.'

Magara was still speaking.

"The General says, Ma'am, that he will call on you later this evening!"

"I quite understand," Theola said.

Her voice was flat and the excitement had gone from her eyes.

The battle was over as far as she was concerned, and she was sure that she had been defeated.

CHAPTER SIX

"You have eaten nothing, Ma'am," Magara said when she came to clear the table at which Theola had sat for her dinner.

"I am not hungry," Theola answered.

"But you should be, Ma'am," Magara insisted. "You had little to eat yesterday and nothing during the night, and when I brought you some food and wine after you returned home you were so deeply asleep that I didn't like to waken you."

"I am not hungry," Theola repeated.

She knew it was her sense of apprehension and unhappiness which made her feel as if her throat was closed and it was impossible to swallow.

She rose from the table to walk to the window.

Once she had felt constricted in the Palace and thought it dull to look out onto the formal gardens; but now she wanted nothing more than to go on living here, to be close to Alexius Vasilas, to have a part in his plans for the future of Kavōnia.

She heard Magara leave the room but did not turn round.

Outside, the sun was sinking in a blaze of glory, and yet it seemed to Theola as if it were already dark, a darkness which struck into her very heart.

And yet insistent in her mind was the rapture and the ecstasy she had felt when the General had kissed her.

She had only to remember it to feel the flames of a fire stir within her, and her lips quivered with the need for his.

'I love him! I love him!' she thought despairingly, 'but I will never mean anything to him but a . . . figure-head.'

The thought that he might love the Princess Athene, of whom Magara had spoken, was like a sword piercing her.

What was the Princess like? Was she beautiful? Was she perhaps his ideal woman, as Theola could never be?

She tortured herself with imagining that the Princess looked Greek, like Alexius Vasilas himself.

Perhaps she was the perfect Aphrodite to his Apollo, and that was the woman he had wanted at his side when he ruled over Kavōnia.

She could understand how easy it had been for him to substitute in the people's minds herself for Catherine, whom the Prime Minister had been clever enough to connect with the legend.

Her father had said she looked like a nymph, and in her wedding-gown to the peasants she must have appeared the embodiment of all their yearnings.

'It was all a clever, theatrical performance,' Theola thought, and the mysticism of what she had felt then, and when she had prayed for the General in the cave, seemed to fade away.

Now she felt flat and deflated, a girl of no importance, someone whom her Aunt had described as "little better than a servant."

The sun went down.

There was that exquisite moment of dusk when the shadows seemed full of secrets and the statues were still silhouetted white against the encroaching darkness.

But Theola could only see Alexius Vasilas's handsome face, his broad forehead, straight nose, the firmness of his chin, and his eyes looking into hers.

What did he think? What were his feelings? He would always remain an enigma, she thought, a man she would never understand.

There was a sharp knock on the door and she turned round, her heart giving a frightened leap, and found it difficult to tell whoever was there to enter.

She spoke in Kavōnian, and the door opened and she saw the General. Because she was so glad to see him she could scarcely prevent herself from running towards him.

Then, incredibly, he was followed by two soldiers.

They came into the room, shut the door behind them, and stood stiffly to attention on sentry duty inside the Sitting-Room rather than outside in the corridor.

Theola stared at them in bewilderment, then raised her eyes questioningly.

The General came a little way towards her to stand still in the centre of the room, and she could not understand the expression on his face.

"I wish to talk to you," he said in English.

"I have been . . . waiting for you to . . . come to me," she answered. "But why are these soldiers here?"

"I have brought them so that you will feel safe," he said.

"Safe from . . . what?" Theola asked in astonishment.

131

"From myself!" he replied.

She could hardly credit what he had said before he continued:

"I abused your trust in me last night. Today I am making sure that it will not happen again."

"I do not . . . understand."

"I think you do," he replied, "and what I have to say will not take long."

Suddenly she understood.

He was referring to the fact that he had kissed her before he left the cave, and because his attitude overwhelmed her to the point where she thought she would cry, she said quickly:

"Send the soldiers away! I will not speak to you while they are in the room!"

The General was still.

"Are you wise to ask this?" he asked.

Because she thought her eyes might be too revealing, Theola turned and walked towards the window.

"Send them . . . away!" she said again, and heard her voice trembling on the words. "I consider . . . their presence an . . . insult!"

"I did not mean it to be one."

The General dismissed the soldiers and Theola heard them leave the room and shut the door.

She stood looking out into the twilight and felt as if the quiet garden were slipping away into an impenetrable future that was somehow horribly menacing.

"I have come to tell you," she heard him say behind her, "that I have learnt there is an English ship in Khévea. A carriage will be waiting within the hour to convey you to it."

For a moment Theola thought she was paralysed and would never be able to move again. Then slowly she turned round from the window.

She had never seen him look so stern and there was an almost grey look about his face.

"A . . . ship?" she repeated.

"An English ship. It may be going to Athens, in

132

which case you can join your Uncle and cousin; or if it is sailing straight to England, it will take you safely home."

Theola found it difficult to understand what she was hearing.

She had supposed he did not care for her, but she could not believe that he would dispose of her so quickly that her departure would take place within an hour.

She stood staring at him, and just as a drowning man's whole life passes before his eyes as he is sinking, so Theola saw the future awaiting her in England: the bleakness of the Castle, the life of fetching and carrying, always surrounded by an atmosphere of hatred.

It had been hard enough to endure before, but now it would seem intolerable when she must leave her heart behind her in Kavōnia.

She had vaguely imagined that it would be difficult to live with her love, knowing Alexius Vasilas did not love her, but it would be infinitely harder to live far away from him in England, knowing she would never see him again.

As if his voice came from a long distance she heard him say:

"I must thank you for all you have done for Kavōnia, but I am sure I am doing what is right in sending you back to your own people."

"I . . . I thought . . . we were . . . married," Theola faltered.

"I can deal with the Civil Marriage," he answered, "and although it will take time I am certain we can obtain an annullment from the Church, seeing that you were constrained into marriage without thought or preparation."

'He has thought of everything,' she thought despairingly.

Then, when it seemed as if he was about to leave, she said:

"Please . . . let me stay."

She thought he stiffened before he replied:

"You must realise that is impossible."

"But why? I will be no . . . trouble. I will make no . . . demands upon you, but I could perhaps . . . work among the people."

"It is not a practical suggestion."

His tone was hard.

"Until you have a hospital," Theola said frantically, "I could tend the sick, especially the children."

"It is best for you to return to the life you know. You have no idea what difficulties and dangers the future may hold."

"I am not . . . afraid. I came with you . . . last night."

"It was very brave of you. But another time we might not be so fortunate."

"Another time?" Theola questioned. "Is there any chance of the King attacking us again? You have their guns and I cannot believe that his few soldiers remaining alive could now prove a menace to your own Army."

"I was not thinking of the King's forces," Alexius Vasilas answered, almost as if he had been goaded into a reply. "There are other difficulties."

"Tell me . . . what they . . . are."

"There is no point in this discussion," he said. "Besides, time is passing. You will wish to pack, and it is a two-hour drive to Khévea."

"Surely it is too late . . . at night to go . . . all that . . . long way?" Theola suggested bleakly.

"I will send a detachment of the Cavalry with you, with Major Petlos in charge of them."

Theola did not answer and after a moment he said:

"I will of course bid you farewell when you are ready to leave."

He turned towards the door and she gave a little cry.

"I cannot . . . go! Please . . . let me . . . stay! There is so . . . much I can do here!"

"No!"

The monosyllable seemed to ring out harshly and echo round the room.

"I have said I will be no . . . trouble to . . . you. I would not expect even to live in the Palace, if you do not . . . want me. But let me . . . stay in Kavōnia!"

"No!"

Theola felt as if her control was breaking. She could feel the tears rising in her throat and choking her.

She saw Alexius Vasilas walk towards the door and she thought wildly that he was going out of her life forever. With him would go the light, so that for the rest of her life she would be in darkness.

He turned the handle.

"I have . . . something to . . . ask you."

Her voice was hardly above a whisper, and she feared he had not heard her.

"What is it?"

She could not believe a question could sound so indifferent, so hard, so cold and distant.

"So that I . . . shall have . . . something to . . . remember, will you . . . will you . . . kiss me . . . good-bye?"

For a moment she thought he was going to refuse.

There was the whole length of the room between them, and when he turned it was impossible, because her eyes were filled with tears, to see the expression on his face.

Very slowly, step by step, he walked back towards her.

She heard rather than saw him coming, and now her heart was thumping frantically in her breast and her lips were trembling with the anticipation of feeling his.

It would be, she thought unhappily, the last kiss she would ever know, the only joy she would have to remember in the years ahead.

"Why do you ask me such a thing?" he asked.

There was a strange note in his voice that had not been there before.

He was still standing several feet from her.

She tried to look at him but it was impossible to do so.

Instead, she closed her eyes, and raising her face a little she said in a voice he could hardly hear:

"Please . . . kiss me . . . please . . ."

It was a plea that came from the very depths of her being and she thought as he did not move that he would reject her.

Then suddenly he moved not to take her in his arms but to reach out his hand and take hold of one of hers.

"Come!"

He pulled her forward, and to her astonishment Theola found herself moving across the room beside him.

He opened the door and they passed the sentries.

Now they were walking so swiftly that Theola could hardly keep up with him down the corridor towards the Grand Staircase.

He did not relinquish her hand, and she had to hold up the skirt of her pink gown with the other in case she should trip from the speed at which he was taking her down the stairs.

They reached the front door and as he passed through it the sentries came to attention.

Still holding her hand, he drew her down the steps to where at the foot of them there was an open carriage.

He helped her into it, gave an order to the driver, and the horses set off at a sharp pace while Theola sat back, breathless and bewildered.

What was happening? Why was he behaving like this? Could he really be sending her to the ship just as she was, without changing her clothes, without any luggage?

She wanted to ask him what was happening, but

her unshed tears still choked her and everything seemed to be swimming in front of her eyes.

All she could be sure of was that he was near her; yet he had not kissed her as she had asked.

'It was . . . immodest of me to . . . suggest such a . . . thing,' she thought.

She knew that in refusing her request he had shut the door of Heaven in her face.

'There is . . . nothing more I . . . can do,' she thought.

She had begged him to let her stay and she had failed. She had asked for his lips and he had refused her even that last moment of happiness.

Now he was sending her away and she had nothing more to say, no further appeal she could make.

The carriage suddenly came to a standstill. Theola opened her eyes, blinked, and saw that they were outside a white Villa.

There were high cypress trees round it and in the gathering dusk it looked very beautiful.

A servant ran to open the door of the carriage and Alexius Vasilas stepped out.

He took Theola's hand to help her to the ground and she felt herself quiver because he was touching her again.

He drew her inside the house and she had a quick impression of a hall with white walls and soft lights which came from alabaster vases.

Still without speaking, he drew her into a Sitting-Room that had long windows opening onto a garden.

Here too there were soft lights and the room gave the impression of being cool, white, and somehow exquisite.

But Theola had no time to look round her. Her eyes were turned irresistibly towards the man with her.

She heard the door close behind them. Then he relinquished her hand to stand looking at her but not far away, in fact close enough for her to tremble because of his very proximity.

His eyes were on her face but he did not speak and after a moment she said:

"Why . . . have you . . . brought me . . . here? W-where . . . are we?"

"I want you to ask me again what you asked me in the Palace," he said. "I am not certain I heard you correctly."

There was a note in his voice which made something stir within Theola's breasts, and now again it was hard to speak—but for a different reason.

He did not move and she knew he was waiting.

"I . . . asked you to . . . kiss me," she whispered.

"Are you sure that is what you want?"

He came a little nearer as he spoke.

Once again she lifted her face to his and knew that she wanted his lips more than she had ever wanted anything in her whole life.

Very slowly he put his arms round her, almost as if he expected her to protest.

Then his lips came down on hers and she felt the rapture streak through her as she had felt it the night before. But now it was even more intense, more wonderful, and more glorious than she had remembered.

She moved closer and still closer to him, wanting her body to melt into his, to become a part of him.

As she did so she felt flames of fire flicker through her and with them came a light which was almost blinding in its intensity.

"I love . . . you! I love . . . you!" she wanted to say, and wished as he swept her up into the sky that she could die.

Nothing in Heaven could be more wonderful, more ecstatic, more perfect than the feelings that made her quiver in his arms and respond to his lips with every fibre of her being.

She forgot everything, even her own unhappiness, even her fear of the future.

She was a part of him and she felt as if a fire within them both consumed everything but their love. . . .

It might have been centuries later that Alexius

Vasilas raised his head and looked down into her eyes.

"Is that what you wanted?" he asked, and his voice was unsteady.

She felt dazed by the emotions through which she had passed.

At the same time, it was an inexpressible agony to know that the wonder she had experienced had come to an end.

His lips were very near hers and she waited, longing once more for the touch of them but afraid to ask.

"Why did you want me to kiss you?" he asked.

The question seemed to come to her from another world.

"I love . . . you!" she whispered. "Please . . . let me . . . stay in . . . Kavōnia."

His arms tightened round her until she gave a little cry with the sheer pain of it.

"Do you really think I could let you go?"

"You were . . . sending me . . . away."

"Only because I had failed your trust."

"I do not . . . understand."

"When I proposed that our marriage should be in name only, I knew that it would be hard for me not to touch you, not to make you mine," he said, "but I believed I could control myself."

He gave a sigh.

"I found that I am just as unrestrained and unreliable as the soldier whom I shot because he assaulted you."

"You . . . you wanted me . . . even before we were . . . married?" Theola asked incredulously.

"I loved you from the first moment I saw you!"

"You looked at me with . . . contempt!"

"Only because I associated you with the people you were with," he answered. "But that did not prevent my thinking you were the most beautiful woman I had ever seen in my whole life."

"That cannot be . . . true!" Theola cried, remembering how drab she must have appeared in the ugly travelling-gown which her Aunt had chosen for her.

Alexius drew her a little closer.

"I knew as we carried the child into that house that something strange had happened to me. It was not only your beauty which held me, but your spirit which reached out towards mine. As I slipped away from the soldiers I knew that somehow, in some way, I must see you again."

"You did not . . . expect to find me . . . left behind in the . . . Palace?" Theola asked.

"I was astonished," he replied, "and at the same time glad in a manner that seemed to surpass every other feeling, even the joy of having at long last been strong enough to lead a revolution against the Austrians!"

"I never thought . . . I never dreamt that you might . . . love me."

"And now you know I do!"

He did not wait for an answer but sought her lips, and she felt the room spin round them and disappear.

There was only the light, the light she knew came from Apollo himself.

He was carrying her away into a wonder for which there were no words, only a glory which belonged to the gods.

* * *

In the garden the nightingales were singing.

Through the open window Theola could see the moon, which had shone over the valley last night when she had prayed for the success of the battle.

Her prayers had been answered, and now it seemed to her that no-one could be so happy and still be upon earth.

"I love you, my darling!"

Alexius's deep voice made her lift her face to his and she felt his lips against her forehead and then her cheeks.

"I did not believe anyone could be so soft, so sweet, so utterly perfect!" he said. "Do you still love me?"

"I love you . . . beyond words," she answered. "I thought when you first . . . kissed me it would be . . . impossible to feel more intensely, but now . . ."

"Now?" he prompted.

She hid her face against his neck.

"I am . . . afraid!" she whispered.

"Of what?"

"That I am dreaming . . . that I shall wake up to find you are not here."

"I promise you that will not happen," he assured her. "You belong to me, Theola, you are my wife and nothing and no-one will ever part us."

"You really . . . love me?"

"It will take me all eternity to tell you how much!" he answered. "You are everything I have always longed for and never found, the sacred ideal that has always been enshrined in my heart and which I had begun to believe was only an illusion."

There was a depth in his voice that made her draw in her breath. Then Theola said:

"You must not . . . say . . . that. It makes me feel just as I did . . . when the soldiers . . . kissed my hands and the women the . . . hem of my gown. That I am . . . inadequate."

"You could never be that!"

"How can you be . . . sure?"

"Because you are the nymph who came from the foam, and because we have recognised each other not only with our eyes, my precious, but with our hearts and our souls."

"How could . . . you have . . . sent me . . . away?"

The hurt of it still remained in her voice even though she knew she now belonged to him.

"I was so ashamed of my behaviour," he said. "I thought I must have shocked and disgusted you. The only reparation I could make was to send you home."

"There is no . . . home for me in . . . England . . ." she began.

She thought as she spoke that she had not yet told him about her father.

There was in fact so much they had to say to each other, so many explanations to be made.

But when she would have begun, she felt his hand touch her and she quivered with new sensations she had never felt before.

"I love you!" Alexius said. "I love you so overwhelmingly, so completely, that it will be hard, my sweet dream, even to think of all I must do in Kavōnia when I shall be thinking of you."

It was impossible for her to answer because once again his lips were seeking hers, and flames of fire were flickering through her body and igniting a passionate desire which was an aching need.

"You are like . . . Apollo," she whispered. "I thought it when I first . . . saw you, and I know now . . . that you are the god of light."

He was kissing her neck and she said, her voice coming in fitful gasps:

"My . . . father told me that he . . . conquered by the power of his . . . beauty and . . . love."

"Is that how I have conquered you?"

"Yes! . . . Yes! . . . Oh yes!"

There was no more need for words.

* * *

Theola awoke from a dream in which she was being kissed and found that it was reality.

Alexius was bending over her and his lips were on hers.

She opened her eyes and found that the room was filled with sunshine.

Outside, there was the song of the birds and she could hear the soft, cool sound of water falling from a fountain into the stone basin beneath it.

"You look very beautiful in the morning, my darling," Alexius said, and she saw that he was already dressed.

"You are . . . leaving me?"

It was a cry of distress.

142

"I have to go to work, my precious. That is what men are saying all over the world at this moment. For me this morning it is especially true."

"Why did you not . . . wake me when you . . . rose?"

"You were sleeping like a child, and I have never seen anything as lovely as your face."

Theola lifted her arms to push back her hair and as she did so the bed-clothes slipped down and she realised she was naked.

Hastily she pulled up the sheet, the colour rising in her cheeks.

"I . . . have no . . . clothes!"

"Magara will have brought you some," he said with a smile, "but I love you just as you are!"

"You are not to . . . look at me, it makes me feel . . . shy!"

"You are my wife, and nymphs traditionally wear very little."

Deliberately Alexius pulled aside the sheet and kissed her breasts one after the other. Then he kissed her lips and she saw the fire in his eyes.

"I want you! God knows I want you!" he said. "But if I do not leave now the people will think their new Ruler is very dilatory."

He stood up and looked down at her to say:

"If I had the choice, I would stay here all day making love to you, telling you how exquisite you are and how perfect in every way. But as it is I have to choose a new Government and appoint many people to positions of responsibility."

He turned away as if it was an effort.

Theola reached out her arms.

"Kiss me . . . once more," she pleaded.

He turned back to kiss her fiercely and passionately. Then as he felt her lips respond and her whole body vibrate against him, he kissed her eyes, saying:

"You are not to tempt me, Theola! If you only knew how hard it is for me to leave you."

He kissed the tip of her nose and said:

"As soon as I have created some semblance of order

143

we will go away on our honeymoon. I want to take you to my hut in the mountains where I have lived these past years. It is very primitive, but I shall have you alone."

"That is what I would like," Theola cried, "to be ... alone with you. Can we really go there?"

"As soon as I can, my dearest heart, my lovely perfect little wife."

He set her back against the pillows and walked resolutely towards the door.

"When shall I see you?" she asked, and it was a cry.

"At luncheon-time," he replied. "Even the busiest man is entitled to a break at midday."

He smiled at her irresistibly and then he was gone.

Theola gave a sigh of sheer happiness and turned her face towards the window.

She had learnt during the night where they were.

The Villa belonged to the family of Nicias Petlos. When Alexius and his mother were exiled from Kavōnia they had collected the treasures of the Vasilas family and installed them in their own house.

Nicias Petlos's father had saved King Ferdinand's life when he first came to Kavōnia, from an anarchist's bomb which had been thrown into his carriage.

Colonel Petlos had picked it up and thrown it into the roadway before it exploded.

King Ferdinand had been understandably grateful.

When all the other Kavōnian officers and dignitaries in the Palace were dismissed, Colonel Petlos and later his son had been kept in office and allowed privileges to which no other Kavōnian was entitled.

The Petlos family had, however, become appalled at the manner in which the King behaved once he had the power.

Colonel Petlos resigned his appointment after several years, giving the excuse that he was too old to continue. But his son, on the insistence of Alexius Vasilas, who had returned secretly to the country, had remained in office, believing this to be the best way he could help Kavōnia.

"Tomorrow I will show you many treasures of my family which have been handed down for generation after generation," Alexius said to Theola.

"I would love to see them."

"They would have been destroyed had it not been for the kindness of my friends."

"You will reward Major Petlos?" Theola asked.

"I intend that he shall take over the training of the Army," Alexius said. "He is young for such an important position, but I know I can rely on him. Although I hope Kavōnia will never have to fight again, we must always be in a position to defend ourselves."

"I cannot . . . bear to think you . . . might ever again be in . . . danger," Theola said.

"The only danger at the moment," Alexius answered, "is that I shall love you so much that you will get bored with me."

"That will . . . never happen," she whispered. "All I want is to be with . . . you."

"We will be together every day," Alexius said, "and at night you will sleep here in my arms."

"Here?"

"This will be our home."

"Is that why you brought me here tonight?" Theola asked. "I could not understand why you were taking me away from the Palace."

"Do you think I could kiss you or make love to you in the place that has been built with the tears and misery of my people?" he asked. "On one thing I am determined—we will never live there!"

"I would much . . . rather be . . . here."

"The Petloses have given it to me until I can build a house of my own, or perhaps it would be wisest to buy it from them."

He drew her closer as he said:

"For the moment those decisions are unimportant. All that matters, my beloved little wife, is that I have somewhere to make love to you."

His lips held her captive and her body moved against his.

* * *

"When are you going to be proclaimed King?" Theola asked very much later.

Her voice was nervous as she asked the question. The very idea of Alexius becoming so grand made her apprehensive.

"Never!"

"Never?"

"No. I think Kavōnia has had enough of the might of Monarchs. We will be an independent Republic."

"But what will . . . you be?"

"President, and I shall be very democratic! It is, I believe, what is wanted in the world today!"

He paused.

"Do you mind not being a Queen, my precious?"

"I want only to be your . . . wife."

"As you are and always will be!"

He kissed her and it was some time before Theola could ask:

"What will you do with the Palace?"

"One wing of it will become a hospital until I can afford to build a new one," Alexius answered. "The other wing will be offices. Only the centre will be kept for entertaining visitors from other countries and for the few occasions when we must give a Reception or, perhaps much later, when the country is prosperous, a Ball."

He pulled her to him so that their bodies touched as he said:

"I would like to dance with you, my adorable little wife, but for the moment I am very content to hold you close to me like this, with only the beating of our hearts for music."

His words came back to her as Theola sat up in bed and saw her pink evening-gown thrown untidily over a chair, her slippers scattered on the floor as well as what her Aunt would have referred to as "unmentionable garments."

She blushed as she remembered how the fire blaz-

ing within them both had swept away every thought
but the need they had of each other.

"I love him! Thank You . . . thank You . . . God . . .
for his love," Theola cried. "And thank You for giving
me this . . . perfect, inexpressible . . . happiness."

As she prayed there was a knock at the door and
Magara came in.

"You are awake, Ma'am?" she asked unnecessarily.
Theola smiled.

"I am awake, Magara, and very, very happy!"

"I thought you would be, Ma'am, when I learnt the
General had brought you here."

"It is so beautiful," Theola said, looking round the
room, "and very different from the Palace."

The contrast was extraordinary.

The bed-room was all white and so was the bed.
There was no heavy canopy over it like the beds at
the Palace, but instead an exquisitely carved head-
board of cupids and dolphins embellished with silver.

Theola was certain that it was native work, just as
the mats which covered the floor were white with
coloured patterns which she had seen in pictures of
Greek crafts.

The curtains were hand-woven in brilliant colours.

The rooms seemed to blend into the flower-filled
garden through the wide open windows opening onto
it.

The scent of roses and lilies was almost overpowering, and as Theola dressed Magara told her she had
ordered her breakfast to be served outside on the
patio which opened out of the Sitting-Room.

"I hope you have brought me a gown to wear,"
Theola said.

"One of your prettiest and coolest, Ma'am," Magara
replied. "I will bring your other gowns here later.
There was no time this morning to order a carriage."

"I am so glad we can live here."

"It is very small after the Palace," Magara answered,
"but easy to run, and the servants will be very
honoured that they can wait on you."

It would be impossible, Theola thought as she sat on the patio under the shade of a canopy, to feel any happier!

All she wanted was to be with Alexius, to look after him, to know that they belonged to each other and she was no longer alone.

After all she had suffered, after all her misery, it was like being swept from the depths of Hell into Heaven itself to know that she was his wife and that he needed her as she needed him.

'I must help him in every way,' Theola thought. 'There is so much I can do for the women of Kavōnia, and of course the children.'

She thought that as soon as Alexius would let her she would call on the little girl whose leg was injured, and she would also find out what had happened to the children who had been in the Palace.

She was sure their mothers would have collected them; but she must discover if their injuries were healed or if they still needed medical attention.

'All these things must be my responsibility,' she thought. 'Alexius will have so many more-important things to do that he must not be worried with lesser problems.'

When she had finished breakfast she walked into the garden, finding it far more beautiful than the formal, statue-embellished gardens of the Palace.

There were azaleas in brilliant colours, lilies which made her think of the sanctity of the Cathedral, and orchids in every shape and colour, many of them growing wild.

There was a water-garden with a little cascade running over artificial rocks, and in the basin of the fountain there were goldfish gliding under the flat green leaves of the water-lilies.

'It is a place for love,' Theola thought, and realised she had wandered round the garden for a long time.

It would be getting near midday. Her heart leapt at the thought that Alexius would be returning to her.

She knew that the moment he appeared she would

be able to run into his arms as she had wanted to do when he had come into her room at the Palace last night and brought the sentries with him.

Supposing she had been forced to obey him, and instead of being here now waiting for his return, she had been on the English ship sailing towards Athens to find her Uncle and Catherine waiting for her?

She felt herself shiver at the thought, then told herself she had no more to fear.

Nothing need ever frighten her again.

She belonged to Alexius and like Apollo he brought the light into the darkness of her existence, and as her father had said, it was a "dancing, quivering flame."

She moved back through the open windows into the cool, white Sitting-Room.

There were pictures on the walls which she had not yet had time to examine, but she knew they would be beautiful because they belonged to Alexius's family.

She thought she would look closely at one and as she moved towards it the door opened. One of the servants said in Kavōnian:

"A gentleman to see you, Ma'am."

Theola turned round, then stood transfixed.

It was the Duke who was entering the Sitting-Room and following him was Catherine!

CHAPTER SEVEN

Theola stood frozen into immobility.

"Oh, here you are, Theola!" the Duke remarked.

"I did not . . . expect to see . . . you, Uncle . . . Septimus!" Theola faltered.

He seemed so large and overpowering that she felt herself once again being dominated by his dislike of her, which seemed to emanate from him like a vibration of evil.

"I dare say not!" the Duke said. "But I am returning to England immediately, and Catherine and I have called to collect you."

"To . . . collect me?" Theola exclaimed.

"We are on our way to Khévea," the Duke explained, "where, thank God, there is a British ship

which will carry us to safety. Hurry and get ready!
There is no time to lose!"

The last word of his sentence was drowned by a
sudden scream from Catherine.

She had entered the room behind him and had
been looking round her and until this moment had not
even glanced at Theola.

Now she cried:

"That is my gown you are wearing! How dare you
wear my clothes! Take it off immediately! Do you
hear?"

She walked towards Theola, who was, however,
looking at her Uncle.

"I . . . I have . . . something to tell you, Uncle
S-Septimus."

"What is it?" the Duke asked sharply.

"I . . . am . . . married!"

If she had meant to surprise him she had certainly
succeeded.

He stared at her as if he could not believe his ears,
then asked:

"To whom? And how could you have married since
we left here?"

"I am the . . . wife of . . . General Vasilas!"

It seemed for a moment as if the Duke could not
take in the full implication of what she had said. Then
his voice seemed to roar round the room as he shouted:

"Vasilas? The revolutionary? The man who has
ousted the King and plunged this wretched country
into blood-shed? You must be mad!"

Theola did not answer. She was only trembling, her
eyes on her Uncle's face.

"I suppose he compelled you," he said grudgingly,
"although I am surprised he offered you marriage.
However, it is not valid; for as you well know, at your
age you cannot be married without your guardian's
permission. That, as I have told you before, is something I will never give. Leave this to me and get ready.
We are departing for England immediately!"

"I . . . I cannot . . . g-go with . . . you!"

Theola tried to speak bravely, but her voice trembled.

"You will do as you are told," the Duke said. "Unless you wish me to use more-forcible arguments."

"She is wearing my gown, Papa," Catherine cried, "and making use of my things! Punish her! She has no right to behave in such a way!"

"Theola will be punished when we get away from here," the Duke answered. "Make no mistake about that! In the meantime, if we are to reach Khévea we must leave."

He pulled a watch from his pocket.

"You have twenty minutes in which to pack your things."

"And I want mine packed," Catherine interposed. "All of them! And do not forget, Papa, Mama's tiara is still here."

"I had not forgotten," the Duke answered.

He put his watch back into his pocket and realised that Theola had not moved.

"Are you refusing to do as you have been told, Theola?" he asked.

Now he spoke slowly, and she knew of old there was something very ominous in the artificial quietness of his voice.

"I . . . I must . . . stay with my . . . husband."

The words came jerkily from between her lips because she was trembling.

The Duke raised his hand and she braced herself for the inevitable blow on the side of the head that she had received so often before.

At that moment the door opened.

Major Petlos appeared and the Duke lowered his arm.

"How nice to see Your Grace again," Major Petlos said in a affable tone.

"It is Petlos, is it not?" the Duke enquired.

"It is, Your Grace. You will remember I travelled

153

with you in the ship which brought you to Khévea."

"I remember you," the Duke said ungraciously, "although I cannot understand why you are still here."

"Everything will be explained if Your Grace and Lady Catherine will accompany me to the Palace," Major Petlos replied. "I have a carriage outside."

"And we have ours," the Duke replied.

"Of course," Major Petlos conceded. "You are on your way to Khévea, I believe."

"That is correct," the Duke answered.

"Then will Your Grace come with me?" Major Petlos asked, a note of authority in his voice.

"I think we just have time," the Duke conceded.

He looked again at Theola.

"And you do as you are told," he said. "If you are not ready by the time I return, it will be very much the worse for you."

He started to follow Major Petlos from the Sitting-Room but Catherine turned back.

"Take off my gown immediately!" she hissed at Theola. "And if you are wearing my petticoats and silk stockings, take them off too! How dare you presume to steal my clothes?"

She paused and there was a very vindictive note in her voice as she added:

"I promise you I will see to it that not only Papa, but also Mama, punishes you severely for the manner in which you have behaved. It is disgraceful!"

She flounced from the room, not waiting for Theola to reply, and as she disappeared in her sapphire-velvet riding-habit, Theola put her hands up to her eyes.

How could she have imagined for one moment that her happiness would last and that she could stay in Kavōnia as Alexius's wife?

She might have known that the magical wonder of last night was but a transitory joy.

Now she had to face reality and she knew only too well how her Uncle would punish her for what he thought of as her misdeeds.

It had been an agony and an humiliation to be whipped by him before, but now she thought it would be utterly unbearable simply because she had known real happiness.

But worse than being punished, worse than the misery and the darkness awaiting her in England, was the thought that she must leave Alexius behind.

She was sure that her Uncle had spoken the truth when he said that her marriage was not valid because she had not the permission of her guardian.

She expected too that he would take the opportunity of telling Alexius about her father and make him believe that she was not a fit person to be the wife of any man.

She was aware how ruthless her Uncle could be when he wanted his own way.

Although she believed that Alexius would fight for her, he would not be able to stand up against the power and influence her Uncle could exert in England if he wished to do so.

Theola had the idea that diplomatically he could make things very difficult not only for Alexius himself, but also for Kavōnia.

What was more, she was quite certain he would not hesitate to use every weapon in his power to hurt her.

It was all a personal vendetta, in that he had never forgiven his sister for bringing, as he thought, shame upon the family honour.

Theola felt that every time he looked at her she aroused in him a desire to avenge what he thought of as her father's perfidy.

"Oh, Papa! Papa!" she cried now in her heart. "No-one can save me! No-one!"

Because she realised that time was passing she went into the bed-room to find Magara. Then she remembered that the maid would be at the Palace.

She opened the wardrobe and found that it contained nothing except for the pink gown she had worn last night and the white wrap with the wide sleeves which belonged to Catherine.

Slowly and with a little difficulty, as there was no-one to help her, Theola took off the beautiful gown which she had hoped Alexius would admire.

Underneath it, as Catherine had suspected, she wore the silk petticoats and the exquisitely embroidered lingerie trimmed with real lace that had been part of her cousin's trousseau.

She took them off and with them the silk stockings which, coming from Bond Street, had been extremely expensive.

There was no sign of Magara, although Theola expected her to arrive at any moment. So she put on the white wrapper and sat down to wait.

She was quite certain that, having arrived at the Palace, the Duke had given instructions for Catherine's trunks to be packed, and that was what Magara would be doing at this moment.

When they were ready for the journey she would doubtless bring over the dowdy, shapeless gowns that her Aunt had chosen for her to wear in her capacity as Lady-in-Waiting.

They were symbolic, Theola thought, of the ugliness and the cruelty that was all that would be left to her for the rest of her life.

If her mother had disgusted her Uncle by marrying her father, Theola had done the same.

In marrying without his permission, she too had in his eyes committed a heinous crime for which she would be abused and berated every day for the rest of her life.

"I cannot bear it!" she said aloud.

Without Alexius there was no point in going on living.

She remembered the night before last when in the cave he had given her a pistol, and she had thought that if he was killed she too must die.

She was sure, although he did not say so, that that had been in his mind, for he was well aware what would be her fate if the King's forces were victorious.

'I will die!' Theola thought now. 'What is the point of going on living?'

She knew too that she could not contemplate the physical punishment she would be forced to endure at her Uncle's hands.

"I am a ... coward," she whispered. "A ... coward!"

It was very quiet in the bed-room and yet it seemed as if the tumult within her filled the whole place with the noise of warring Armies.

She felt as if they tore her apart.

One side of her mind was telling her that she must live, whatever suffering she had to endure, the other saying that death was infinitely preferable to a life without love!

She rose to ring the bell and it seemed a long time before there was a knock on the door.

"You rang, Excellency?"

She saw that it was Dinos, the elderly man-servant who brought her breakfast to the patio.

"Yes," she answered. "I wish you to bring me a ... pistol."

"A pistol, Excellency?"

"There must be one somewhere in the Villa."

"I am not sure, Excellency—but I will look."

"Thank you, Dinos."

She saw the surprise in his face, but he was too well trained a servant to question any order he was given.

He went away and again Theola waited and wondered if she would be allowed to say good-bye to Alexius.

Perhaps when her Uncle had denounced her and told him the truth about her antecedents, he would realise he was well rid of her.

She had meant to tell him herself—the words had even come to her lips. But he had kissed her and she had forgotten everything but the wonder and rapture of his love.

Even to think of him touching her made her quiver

with the inexpressible glory of it, and it was agonising to know that he would never possess her again.

"I love . . . him!" she cried despairingly. "Oh, God, how much I love him!"

There was a knock on the door and Dinos appeared, holding a pistol in his hand.

"This is the only one I can find, Excellency."

"That will do," Theola answered.

She took it from him, realising that it was an old weapon and very much heavier than the one Alexius had given her in the cave.

"Is there anything else, Excellency?"

"Not for the moment, thank you."

Dinos went from the room and Theola sat down, holding the pistol in her hand.

Now she could actually feel the metal cold against her fingers and she wondered if she would in fact have the strength of will to pull the trigger.

She had seen a picture somewhere of a man intent on killing himself, pointing a pistol at his forehead.

But she thought she could not bear her face to be so shattered that the last impression Alexius would have of her was one of ugliness.

"If I point it at . . . my heart," she told herself, "I will die . . . and I can only pray that it will be . . . instantaneous."

She glanced at the clock which stood on the chest on the other side of the room and saw that her Uncle had been gone nearly twenty minutes.

Then she knew it would be impossible for Magara to pack up all Catherine's clothes in so short a time.

Even if she had the help of the other maids in the Palace, it would take at least twice as long to fold all the lovely, elaborate gowns and empty the chests of all the silk underclothes which Catherine had bought from the most expensive shops in London.

There would also be shoes, handbags, sun-shades, and bonnets, all to be put in the innumerable trunks and band-boxes which had filled the whole of an empty cabin in the ship.

"What am I waiting for?" Theola asked herself. "When they return to collect me, if I am still alive they will prevent me from . . . killing myself."

She looked down at the pistol and knew that what she intended to do was a sin.

She knew too that it was a cowardly action and that Alexius, who had called her brave, would despise her for being so weak.

It was then that the tears came into her eyes.

She whispered:

"I cannot help it . . . my darling! I cannot go on . . . living without you! If I am dead, at least my body . . . like my heart . . . will be in . . . Kavōnia!"

She thought she heard someone coming and quickly raised the pistol in her hand.

She heard the door open and as it did so she shut her eyes and tried to pull the trigger, but it was stiffer than she had expected.

There was a sudden exclamation and a firm hand pulled the pistol from her grasp and Alexius's arms were round her.

"In God's name, what are you doing? My darling, my sweet, what are you doing?"

Theola gave a gasp, then as he pulled her against him she burst into tears.

"They are . . . taking me . . . away," she sobbed, "I have to . . . leave you. It is no . . . use. Let me die! I c-cannot . . . live without you and our . . . love."

The words were almost incoherent. She felt him kiss her hair and then in a voice that was deep and moved she heard him say:

"How can you be so foolish? So utterly and absolutely ridiculous, my sweet wife? Do you really imagine I would let you go?"

She heard him but thought it could not be true until he turned her face up to his. Then he was kissing first her lips, then the tears that were on her cheeks, and lastly her eyes.

"How could you think for one moment that I would let them take you away from me?"

"Uncle . . . S-Septimus s-said the marriage was not . . . valid because he had . . . n-not given his . . . p-permission."

"Our marriage is not only valid," Alexius replied, "but your Uncle has in fact given his permission—for what it is worth!"

Theola was so surprised that her tears were checked and her eyes opened wide in astonishment.

"Is . . . that . . . true?" she whispered.

"Completely and absolutely true," Alexius assured her. "But how could you do anything so wicked—so terribly cruel—as to try to destroy yourself when you belong to me?"

"I . . . I thought you . . . would no longer . . . want me," Theola stammered.

"How dare you doubt my love!" he said in a tone which was meant to be severe.

But he kissed her as he spoke and she clung to him, finding it difficult to believe what he had said.

"Shall I tell you what happened, my precious?" he asked.

Then before she could reply he exclaimed:

"Why have you taken off your clothes? Why are you wearing nothing but this wrap?"

"C-Catherine . . . ordered me to give her . . . back everything I was . . . wearing," Theola said.

It was difficult to speak, difficult to remember anything except the fact that Alexius had said she was not to leave him.

He looked down at her and smiled.

"Well, it makes things very convenient. I was just thinking it was about time I had a siesta!"

He picked her up in his arms, carried her to the bed, and laid her down on top of it.

Then he took off his tunic and lay down beside her, pulling her into his arms and kissing her until it was difficult for her to breathe.

"Please," Theola said when she could speak. "You must . . . tell me what . . . happened."

"Tell me first that you love me," he commanded.

"I adore . . . you! I love you so . . . overwhelmingly . . . so agonisingly, that I knew . . . I could not go . . . back to England with my . . . Uncle."

"That is something which will never happen, and with any luck, we neither of us will set eyes on him again."

"He has . . . gone?"

"He is on his way to Khévea!"

There was a note of satisfaction in his voice and Theola moved a little closer.

"Tell me! Tell me how you . . . managed it."

"It is really all thanks to Nicias Petlos," Alexius began. "He learnt that your Uncle and your cousin had arrived and were asking for you. When they were sent from the Palace to the Villa, Nicias told me what your Uncle was like and how badly he had treated you when you were on board ship."

He kissed Theola's forehead before he said:

"If I were a less enlightened Ruler, I would have thrown him into a dungeon and given him some of his own medicine!"

"What did you do?" Theola asked.

"Primed by Nicias, who told me the Duke was a snob, an autocrat who respected only pomp and circumstance, we staged a special performance for his benefit."

"What . . . did you . . . do?"

"Nicias kept him waiting in the Queen's Sitting-Room. Then when I was ready he said to your Uncle and Catherine:'His Royal Highness Prince Alexius, Ruler of Kavōnia, will grant Your Grace an audience!' "

Alexius gave a little laugh.

"He said there was no doubt that your Uncle was startled, but before he had time to recover he ushered him, with Lady Catherine, into the King's Sitting-Room."

"Where you were . . . waiting for . . . them?"

"I was waiting," Alexius replied, "covered with decorations, most of which had belonged to my father, and I think a few the King had left behind!"

He gave a little chuckle as he went on:

"I assure you I looked very impressive with two Aides-de-Camp, one on either side of me, also dressed up in everything they could find.

" 'His Grace, the Duke of Wellesbourne, Your Royal Highness, and the Lady Catherine Bournel' Nicias Petlos announced.

"I was signing papers and I deliberately delayed a few seconds before I rose to greet them, and they had to walk the whole length of the room before they reached my desk."

Theola remembered how awe-inspiring the King's Sitting-Room had seemed to her the night the revolution had broken out.

"What . . . happened then?" she asked.

"The Duke asked me, in quite a different tone from what I imagine he had intended, if what you had said was true and I had gone through a form of marriage with you.

" 'Hardly a form, Your Grace,' I replied. 'I have married your niece according to the laws of Kavōnia, and we have also been married by His Holiness the Archbishop.'

" 'The marriage is not legal with my permission,' the Duke said.

" 'In the circumstances it was impossible to ask for it,' I replied.

"There was a pause before he said:

" 'You call yourself "Prince." May I ask if in fact you inherited that title?'

"I looked at him as if I considered the question an insult, and he said quickly:

" 'I wondered in fact if you were any relation to King Alexandros V of Kavōnia, who I understand was a Vasilas?'

" 'I see Your Grace has been reading our history!' I remarked. 'King Alexandros V was my father; and my grand-father was Alexandros IV.'

" 'I had no idea—no idea at all!' the Duke ejaculated.

" 'So you see,' I said sharply, 'I consider myself justified in taking over Kavōnia and ridding my country of the foreigner who has in fact usurped my throne for the last twelve years.' "

"Uncle Septimus must have been . . . astonished!" Theola murmured.

"He was surprised for the moment into silence," Alexius agreed. "Then he said:

" 'You do not know the truth about my niece—I consider it my duty to tell you that she is not a suitable wife for any man.' "

Theola gave a frantic cry.

"I intended to . . . tell you!" she said. "I swear . . . I meant to do so . . . but there . . . was no time."

"It is not important," Alexius said indifferently.

"Not . . . important?"

Theola stared at him as if she thought she had not heard him correctly.

"Of course not," he answered. "In fact, when your Uncle told me what had happened so long ago, I said:

" 'What a pity Mr. Richard Waring is not alive. I would have asked him to help me create a University in Kavōnia!' "

"You do not . . . mind . . . that he was not . . . grand or . . . blue-blooded?"

Alexius smiled at her.

"How could I do anything, my lovely wife, but admire and honour your father?"

Theola gave a sigh which came from the depths of her being as Alexius went on:

"The Duke was too stunned to express himself, and I took the opportunity of saying to your cousin:

" 'Am I to understand, Lady Catherine, that you do not intend to marry King Ferdinand?'

" 'A King without a throne,' she replied, 'and for the moment without a place to lay his head, is hardly an attractive prospect.'

" 'No, of course not,' I remarked.

" 'So I am returning to England,' she went on, 'but

I wish to take back with me the tiara which belonged to my mother and the clothes which were my trousseau.'

"'Your first request is quite easy, Lady Catherine,' I replied.

"I looked towards one of the Aides-de-Camp and he brought me the tiara in its velvet box, which had been quite safe in the Queen's bed-room.

"'I am glad to have this back!' Lady Catherine exclaimed."

"I am sure she had expected that it would be stolen," Theola interposed.

"In Kavōnia we steal nothing!" Alexius smiled. "Except hearts!"

"You . . . have stolen . . . mine," Theola whispered.

He looked down into her eyes and she said with an effort:

"Tell me the . . . rest."

"I then began to bargain with the Duke."

"Bargain with him?" Theola exclaimed in surprise.

"For your clothes, my precious. I adore you as you are now, but I have a feeling you would be somewhat embarrassed if this was all you had to wear."

He pulled the wrap from one white shoulder as he spoke and kissed it.

"What do you . . . mean when you say you . . . bargained with Uncle Septimus?"

"I pointed out to the Duke, and of course to your cousin, that the trousseau had been bought to be worn in Kavōnia.

"'When Lady Catherine returns to England,' I said, 'she may choose a husband among the ruling Princes of Sweden, Norway, Denmark, or even Prussia. In which case the gowns she brought to the Palace here would be much too light to be worn in such cold climates.'

"'What are you suggesting?' the Duke enquired.

"I told him in terms of cash."

"How . . . could you?" Theola cried.

"Nicias had already told me that your Uncle was a

mean and extremely avaricious man," Alexius answered. "I had a feeling, considering there would now be no Royal marriage, he would regret all he had spent on his daughter's adornment."

"And you . . . bought them . . . for me?" Theola asked almost incoherently.

"I think your Uncle was quite pleased with the bargain we struck between us."

"But what did . . . Catherine say?"

"She said she insisted on taking with her to the ship enough clothes to wear until they reached Marseilles."

"And you agreed?"

"Of course!" Alexius said. "I sent for Magara and told her what she was to pack."

"Did that take long?"

"Not long. As soon as the trunk was ready it was placed in the Duke's carriage and they set off with all possible speed towards Khévea."

Theola gave a little sigh of relief.

"I do not . . . like to think that you spent so much . . . money on me," she said humbly. "I know how expensive Catherine's trousseau was."

"If it will relieve your mind," Alexius said, "I have been told that already an Art Dealer has arrived at the Palace hoping to purchase the pictures of the Hapsburg ancestors to sell in Vienna."

"Oh, I am glad you can be . . . rid of them!" Theola cried.

"So am I," Alexius agreed. "I never wish to see their smug faces again!"

"I wonder which gowns Magara packed for Catherine?" Theola murmured.

She was hoping that her wedding-gown had not gone with her cousin. She wanted to treasure it all her life.

"I will let you in on a little secret," Alexius said. "I spoke to Magara in Kavōnian and naturally neither your Uncle nor the girl who had expected one day to become Queen of this country could understand what orders I gave her."

"What were they?"

"I told Magara to pack all the clothes that you had brought to Kavōnia for yourself—just those and no others!"

Theola gave a little gasp and looked up at him incredulously.

"*My* gowns? You gave Catherine . . . those? Oh, Alexius . . . how could you?"

"She can always wear the tiara with them!" he said seriously, but his eyes were twinkling.

Quite suddenly Theola saw the funny side of it.

She could imagine Catherine's fury when the trunk was opened after the ship had sailed and she found the hideous brown merino, the grey batiste, and the cheap travelling-gown that her Aunt had chosen deliberately to make her look unattractive.

Even as Alexius laughed she laughed with him. The sound seemed to mingle with the sunshine coming through the windows.

He pulled her close against him as he said:

"Do you realise, my beautiful little wife, I have never heard you laugh before? It is something you must do more often."

"It was . . . unkind of me . . . but I cannot help it!"

"The Kavōnians laugh a lot when they are happy, and they love a joke. That, my precious dream, is a typical Kavōnian joke."

"It is so funny!" Theola gasped. "Oh, Alexius . . . have they really . . . left?"

"They have really left!" he repeated. "And now tell me how sorry you are that you did not trust me. How could you have imagined for one moment that I would lose you or ever let you leave me now that you are my wife?"

"Forgive me . . . please forgive . . . me," she whispered.

"I will forgive you only if you promise you will never again do anything so wicked and so wrong."

Alexius spoke sternly, and the colour rose in Theola's cheeks.

"I am very . . . sorry, and I . . . promise."

"Fortunately old Dinos has plenty of common sense," Alexius said, "and you would have found it very difficult, my sweet, to kill yourself without a bullet in the pistol!"

"It was not . . . loaded?" Theola asked.

"It was not, my foolish one! And that is another Kavōnian joke!"

Theola laughed a little tremulously.

Even now she could hardly believe that the nightmare was over, the darkness was gone, and once again she was in the light, the blinding, mystical light that always seemed to surround Alexius.

"I love you . . . so desperately," she said. "Please . . . teach me not to be . . . stupid or . . . afraid."

"I will teach you to trust me," Alexius replied, "and to remember that I never give up. Sooner or later I am always the conquerer."

"We must . . . conquer Kavōnia with . . . love," Theola whispered.

"We will do it together, you and I!"

"That . . . is all I . . . want."

"But at the moment," he said, "I have someone to conquer who has been very naughty, but who is, I think, now repentant."

His lips came down on hers. She felt him pulling aside her wrapper and his hand was touching her.

Little flames of fire awoke to flicker through her body.

Then his heart was beating against hers and they were no longer two people but one.

A dancing, quivering light enveloped them.

ABOUT THE AUTHOR

BARBARA CARTLAND, the celebrated romantic author, historian, playwright, lecturer, political speaker and television personality, has now written over 150 books. Miss Cartland has had a number of historical books published and several biographical ones, including that of her brother, Major Ronald Cartland, who was the first Member of Parliament to be killed in the War. This book had a Foreword by Sir Winston Churchill.

In private life, Barbara Cartland, who is a Dame of the Order of St. John of Jerusalem, has fought for better conditions and salaries for Midwives and nurses. As President of the Royal College of Midwives (Hertfordshire Branch), she has been invested with the first Badge of Office ever given in Great Britain, which was subscribed to by the Midwives themselves. She has also championed the cause for old people and founded the first Romany Gypsy Camp in the world.

Barbara Cartland is deeply interested in Vitamin Therapy and is President of the British National Association for Health.

Barbara Cartland

The world's bestselling author of romantic fiction. Her stories are always captivating tales of intrigue, adventure and love.

Barbara Cartland

The world's bestselling author of romantic fiction. Her stories are always captivating tales of intrigue, adventure and love.

☐	A VERY NAUGHTY ANGEL	2107	$1.25
☐	THE CRUEL COUNT	2128	$1.25
☐	CALL OF THE HEART	2140	$1.25
☐	AS EAGLES FLY	2147	$1.25
☐	THE MASK OF LOVE	2366	$1.25
☐	AN ARROW OF LOVE	2426	$1.25
☐	A GAMBLE WITH HEARTS	2430	$1.25
☐	A KISS FOR THE KING	2433	$1.25
☐	A FRAME OF DREAMS	2434	$1.25
☐	THE FRAGRANT FLOWER	2435	$1.25
☐	MOON OVER EDEN	2437	$1.25
☐	THE GOLDEN ILLUSION	2449	$1.25
☐	FIRE ON THE SNOW	2450	$1.25
☐	THE HUSBAND HUNTERS	2461	$1.25
☐	THE SHADOW OF SIN	6430	$1.25
☐	SAY YES, SAMANTHA	7834	$1.25
☐	THE KARMA OF LOVE	8106	$1.25
☐	BEWITCHED	8630	$1.25
☐	THE IMPETUOUS DUCHESS	8705	$1.25

Buy them at your local bookseller or use this handy coupon: